LOOSE IN THE BRIGHT FANTASTIC

info@frayededgepress.com

Loose in the Bright Fantastic

E. B. Moore

Frayed Edge Press
Philadelphia, PA

Copyright 2023 E. B. Moore

Published by Frayed Edge Press in 2023

Frayed Edge Press
PO Box 13465
Philadelphia, PA 19101

http://frayededgepress.com

Cover image by E. B. Moore

Publishers Cataloging-in-Publication Data

Names: Moore, E.B.
Title: Loose in the bright fantastic / E. B. Moore.
Description: Philadelphia, PA : Frayed Edge Press, 2023.
Identifiers: LCCN 2022952253 | ISBN 9781642510478 (pbk.) | ISBN
    9781642510485 (ebook)
Subjects: LCSH: Aging parents -- Fiction. | Dementia -- Fiction. | Families
    -- Fiction. | Older Women -- Fiction. | Boston (Mass.) -- Fiction. | BISAC:
    FICTION / Disabilities. | FICTION / Family Life / General. | FICTION
    / Women.
Classification: LCC PS3563.O674 L66 2023 | DDC 813 M--dc22
LC record available at https://lccn.loc.gov/2022952253

To my family
who kept the lighter side alive

We Can't Overestimate

what it means—a home,

even a shack

under a bridge. A place

that's yours, that you

control,

can close the door—keep

people out

let people in.

Found poem taken from
Good Neighbors
by Nancy Rosenblum

PART I

HOME

THE SIREN CALL

CHAPTER 1

MAGGIE

Friday

Street after street, Maggie rabbits around corners, hurtles down alleys, down avenues, her gray hair wet, fur coattails flapping, feet loud in her husband's oversized wingtips. Wearing his shoes keeps him close. *Dear Dan.* Dear Dead Dan.

A cry on the wind pulls her homeward.

Her breath fogs the air. She squints at signs, at house numbers, at doorways. Heels clatter. The racket ricochets off brick, townhouse after Victorian townhouse, so like her own, their roofs all but invisible in swirls of snow.

My babies! Panic squeezes her chest.

Another alley, another corner, doorway after doorway, and finally, out of the white swirl, her beloved door. Number 5. *Thank heaven.*

Light spills through the etched glass. She pats a pocket of her inside-out mink. *It's warmer this way.* She pats the other pocket. *Damn, no keys.* Up the steps, she jabs the doorbell. Thumb hard at the button, once, twice. She bangs her fists on the glass. "Clair! she shouts, "Rog!"

Nothing.

She cups her eyes with blue-veined hands, and peers through the bevels, past the vestibule, past the hall and curving stairs, to the lights hazy in the distant dining room. Off to the left an orange glow, the living room fire. She bangs harder. The glass could break. *I don't care.*

From inside a shadow approaches, blotting the lights. A blurry face appears, nose to the other side of the glass. *The sitter, yes.* She fiddles with the lock.

The tumbler clicks. The door opens and a tall woman in velvet pants steps back as Maggie, along with a shower of snow, surges in. She stops by the stairs, a hand to the carved newel post. Her eyes half shut, she takes in the scent of wood smoke, and the last of her panic dissolves.

"May I help you?" the woman says.

Maggie recoils. "You aren't the sitter." She flexes cranky knees ready to... "Where's Clair?" Gripping the post, she steadies herself. "What have you done with Rog?"

"I'm sorry," the woman says with unnerving kindness. "We have no Clair here." She rests gentle fingers on Maggie's sleeve.

"And no..." Maggie's voice squeaks, "No Rog?"

From the dining room, strangers at the table stare in silence, forks stopped halfway to their mouths. The woman's words stay soft, "No dear, no Rog." Candles on the table flicker, cold blue at the core.

"Where are they?"

But this table is full of questioning eyes. *What have they done with Grandfather's table?* "And my portraits?" Her ancestors' portraits, they're gone too.

"Come," the woman says. "Sit. It's no night to be out." She leads Maggie into the living room. Maggie's eyes lift to the ceiling medallion. They run along the egg-and-dart moldings she'd reclaimed from years of painted abuse.

She collapses onto a stripy sofa she's never seen. The woman sits beside her and takes her hand. "What's your name, dear?"

This new neighbor, what IS her name? "So good of you to drop by," Maggie says. "You'll love townhouse living. Five floors, running up and down, no need of a gym. See?" She opens her mink coat. "You'd never know I just had a baby." She pats the flat of her belly, covered in rainbow spandex. She frowns at her one-piece outfit.

She's dressed for the gym, not guests. And she hasn't offered the woman a drink. And the people in the dining room; clearly, they expect dinner.

Maggie catches the scent of curry. *Oh hell, the timer didn't go off.* She's up. Her mink falls to the floor. Variegated spandex on full display, she's a flash of electric sunset headed for the kitchen.

Halfway through the dining room, she stops. Dinner's already loaded on their plates.

Her plate, too. It waits at the kitchen end of the table. Her chair, at an angle, invites her to sit. But first…

"Won't you join us?" she says to the woman following at her heels.

At the other end of the table, the man in Dan's seat rises. He slips into the living room. *Just like Dan, on the phone with dinner getting cold.* The others keep staring.

She clutches the top of her chair.

Where's Dan? She looks behind her. "Rog!" She turns to her right.

Twists left. "Clair! CLAIR!"

The woman hooks Maggie's elbow. "Come dear, we'll…"

"No." Maggie wrenches away. "Noooo…."

PART II

THE HOSPITAL

CHAPTER 2

MAGGIE

The Previous Tuesday

A stampede in the corridor shatters the medical quiet. Maggie stiffens. Her door swings and hits the wall, dancing her wits like water flicked on a hot frying pan. She hums to herself. She fingers her white wristband.

Margaret Helmsworth Colton. That's me?

Gripping a plastic fork, she eyes lunch, cold on her tray, and from the hall a group pours in: a woman, two men, a smatter of children, their jackets shed on the floor, their laughter overlapping with the musical tootings of a girl with a trumpet.

Maggie straightens her fork at the left of her plate, knife on the right, sharp side—*could plastic be sharp*— turned in, never out, *make it straight,* anything not to look at those faces she can't quite place.

"Hi Mum," the woman says. Sensible heels click against the floor. Beside her, a little kid in a black mask swirls his bright blue cape.

He stumbles over a bigger boy's outstretched sneaker. "Quit it."

Twice his height, the bigger one in a Bruins jersey muscles the kid against the wall. The kid cocks his little fist and puffs his chest, his yellow shirt sewn with a flash of green lightning. "You're toast."

Hockey-Boy bugs his eyes. "Please, Major Amazing Man," he says full of sarcasm, "Don't hurt me."

"That's Mr. Major to you." The little one stomps on Hockey-Boy's boat-sized Ked.

"Ruffian." The woman swats at the closest rump. Major Amazing dodges.

Maggie's humming rumbles a wall around her as the woman herds her gaggle toward the bed. Maggie slips off the far edge. She retreats to an armchair and presses into a corner by the window, her mattress a buffer of rumpled sheets as she studies Boston out the window.

Red leaves fall to a browning carpet. In the distance, whitecaps riffle the blue river. She blinks and dares a glance across the bed.

The crowd swirls. The dark-haired woman breaks loose. Dark hair... *Dark-haired-Clair. Yes.* Funny how rhymes work. *God bless rhyming.*

Maggie's fog eases, as surprising as when it first socked in, and a tiny peephole opens. Faces and names flood in.

Clair—Maggie's oldest, mother to the crew invading her room. A young woman, yet white strands bloom in the brown waves of hair trimmed neatly at her collar. *How could I misplace Clair?*

Or Roger—that's him, Maggie's son, nothing godly about him despite the high white collar. *Roger-Dodger won't let anyone close.*

He's Marine-stiff in his close-cropped hair and misfit skin. She squints. "Rog?" *My glasses.* Hands up to rub her eyes—"Ah, there they are"—and she levels large frames higher on her nose. *So seventies,* the nurse had laughed. Maggie settles deeper in the chair. "Fashion," she says and smooths her hospital johnny. "You can have it."

"Mmmm." *That's Clair trying not to comment.*

"Make way," shouts the kid with a mask.

Hank—*yes.* Maggie's five-year-old grandson barrels through the crowd. His cape flares. *My hero, Major Amazing Man.*

୨୦ ଓଓ

Way back, he'd snitched her black sleep mask. He had learned the hard way that being invisible and being blind were two different things. His shins took a black-and-blue beating before Maggie cut triangular holes. Sight restored.

ജ‍ൠ

On stubby legs he dodges the bed, clambers onto the deep windowsill, and snuggles up. "Hi, Nana," he whispers, and with his knee, he touches Maggie's crepey arm. He rests his small hand on her shoulder, and together, they look out onto the hospital roofs. "What are we watching, Nana?"

Maggie points to the flat gravel a story below. "Gulls," she says. Legs dangling, the birds drop to the gravel and fight over shreds of refuse. She hates the gulls bickering.

"Hi Mum," says Roger. She frowns, a flash of irritation at her son's collar. His friend, standing beside him, gives a cheery wave. Jeremy is tall, his long hair held back in a low ponytail. His loose sleeve brushes Roger's shoulder, and Roger flinches. He widens the space between them.

ജ‍ൠ

In grade school, it was always Roger and Jeremy, Jeremy and Roger, two Musketeers who never needed a third. They laughed and laughed like drunks propping each other up.

Wrestlers in high school, their touch was official, respectable, they reached for closer holds: an elbow crooked around a neck, a leg lifted and clamped on a stomach. Faces jammed together, they pretzeled their bodies. Sweating. Grimacing. Happy.

Then graduation, and Gill their god-damned neighbor got at them. Something no one would forget. After that, they only looked from a distance, vibration filling the room.

ജ‍ൠ

"Just admit it," says Maggie. "Live a little."

Roger wouldn't dare eat a peach, even seedless. Prufrock taught him nothing.

A muscle in Clair's cheek jumps. "Now, Mum..." Brown circles deepen under her eyes. An absent husband will do that, not to mention Zip the dog, three children, and brother Rog wanting to sleep forever on her futon.

Her plate's full, why worry about me? "I'm not gaga." *Who cares if names drift? They come back. May my car keys do the same.*

They disappeared after she returned hours late from the Big Dig. *I can't control traffic.*

Jeremy, *that's him beside Rog,* says he hates those tunnels. *Dear boy.* He's always on Maggie's side. And better yet, he's crazy for Roger, though *why* is a mystery. Roger feigns blindness in the face of Jeremy's assets.

"He does have nice muffins," she says.

Roger pinks up. "God, Mum, you can't just blurt out whatever pops..."

Maggie's tongue, with a mind of its own, has a way of blabbing secrets. Not that Jeremy's assets in tight jeans are a secret.

"Buns," Clair says. "Muffins are for breakfast."

"Mmmmm." Maggie jacks her right eyebrow. "Delicious." Even her eyebrows betray her, sprouting gray and wild. She used to pluck, but why at seventy-nine? A waste of effort.

Roger, redder still, "Mum, please."

But there's hope yet as she catches him copping a quick glance at those *buns,* his eyelids shutting out longing. A hand to his high turtleneck, he presses down tightly.

"Vermont calls," Jeremy says. "'Extended vacation.'" He glares at Roger and, kneeling on the bed, leans across to kiss Maggie's cheek. "My chariot awaits."

He hugs everyone in the room except Roger, who backs away, and waves from the door. Maggie narrows her eyes at Roger. "What have you done?"

"Don't make it worse, Mum."

"Me?" says Maggie. She tilts her head.

As Roger berates her, his words meld with the kids' voices coursing through the room. She lets herself float, memories scattering.

Those scattered wits, so slippery. So hard to gather. There's a price for slippage, some mortification akin to soiling your underwear.

"Jesus, Mum, what were you thinking?" asks Roger.

"Give it a rest." She, too, can talk teen-speak.

Hank whispers close to her ear, "What we need is a nice cup of tea."

She reels herself in. "Lapsang today?" she asks.

He passes her a Styrofoam cup from the tray-table and takes one himself. "I'll make it strong," he says. She loves the tea's smoky flavor, real or unreal.

Dear Hank—a reader from age three. *Close to Hockey-Boy's level.* An avid YouTuber, Hank watches Suma wrestlers and admires Samurais, so Maggie introduced him to tea ceremonies. *That's my Major Amazing Man.*

From a nonexistent teapot, he pours a steaming stream of nothing into the cups. They each blow and take careful sips, their eyes locked.

"Sasha, Ben," Clair calls from the door. *That's Trumpet-Girl and Hockey-Boy.* "Go wait in the van—*Black, and so like a hearse.* You too, Hank. Your uncle and I have business with Nana."

Maggie groans. "What business?"

"You're lucky," says Roger. "The Inuit set their parents adrift on the ice." He slides his hands together as if in evil anticipation. This is the Roger Maggie loves.

"Too bad, Boy-Chick, no ice on the Charles." She thumbs her nose.

"I'll wait for December," he says.

"Fine, push me off the Pepper Pot." *My favorite bridge.* "Save us all a world of trouble."

CHAPTER 3

CLAIR

Five Years Earlier, The End Begins

Fall into winter—the date grows hazy, but the happening, the nucleus of it, stays etched in Clair's mind with a scalpel's precision.

She did fall that winter, along with her mother Maggie and brother Roger—akin to slipping on black ice, the slick unseen, and flying over backward, legs gyrating; a weightless moment hit with its flash of imminent shatter.

ঙ গ

Maggie was nervous the day of the surgery. Pre-dawn, she bustled in her Cambridge kitchen. She offered bananas and All-Bran, though she herself had to fast.

Clair shook her head. "You shouldn't wait on us." She made coffee while Roger stowed his mother's suitcase in the car. On returning he said, "What's in there, the kitchen sink?"

"Why not?" Maggie gave him a nudge. "*You* won't use it."

"Don't want dishpan hands, now do I?" He returned the nudge.

Clair had washed last night's dishes. At her Lexington house, she often left them mounded in the sink, ever-hopeful that her kids would pitch in. But she never left dishes at her mother's. There, Clair scoured pots and pans, wiped counters, made the kitchen pristine the way Maggie preferred.

Everything ready, they shivered by the front door. The grandfather clock tolled five times. The ship on the clock's face rocked, making them all a little seasick.

Maggie picked stray lint off of the Oriental runner and drifted back to the dining room. She brushed a nonexistent crumb from her grandfather's cherry table, nodded at the surrounding gold-framed portraits. On her way through the living room filled with books, she stopped by the fireplace, breathing in the homey whiff of wood smoke. With both hands, she straightened the already straight frame over her mantle, and studied the Hudson River flowing peacefully through its majestic landscape. She took a deep breath. "No sense putting it off."

ജ൫

The problem had started simply, an odd moment not worth mentioning. Maggie had been in a circle of friends, and stopped talking mid-sentence, a three-second loss of speech, of motion, a blank that the ladies ignored or didn't notice in the pouring of tea and the passing of watercress sandwiches. Three seconds, not alarming until she thought of what those frozen moments could mean behind the controls of her high-finned Oldsmobile.

ജ൫

In the hospital, from early morning stiff into the evening, Clair and Roger waited on plastic chairs, their red-shot eyes fixed on the swinging doors where the surgeon promised to emerge with news.

The chairs creaked. Roger massaged his corduroy-covered knees. The PA system squealed, and in it, Clair heard the surgeon's highspeed saw, smelled the spin of acrid smoke, saw her mother's brain laid bare.

Another check of the time.

The waiting room emptied to a sea of abandoned chairs. Finally the surgeon appeared, his scrubs changed to black pants and a starched white coat. "Success," he said. "We took out the tumor and a spot of necrosis." Success, that's what counted.

Next day in the ICU, Clair stood by the bedside. Her mother's body stretched long on the bed, sheet to the chin. A gauze

18

helmet canted over one eye; the rest of her face bruised beyond recognition.

A spaghetti of wires attached her to boxes. Graphs leapt and dropped and leapt again, charting bodily functions along with Clair's hopes. Under fluorescence, she winced at the tubes threading the body's every orifice. Tubes to bags of fluid suspended on poles, and below the bedrail. One bag hung heavy with dark collection. Hesitant breath teased the silence.

"Why doesn't she wake?" Clair rubbed her forehead.

A red light blinked. Alarm flooded the cubicle. "Nurse," Clair's voice a croak. Roger loud with panic, "Come quick."

A zing of ball bearings and a nurse—flowered pinafore over whites—swished the curtain aside. At the end of its runner, the curtain collapsed in folds against the bedside table. The nurse glanced at Maggie's wristband. "Right." She poked a button on the offending box. The warning went silent.

"She's fine." The nurse gave a reassuring smile, and the curtain swished closed again. There was never a hint of Maggie's metamorphosis. Not a clue to the fracas lying in wait.

CHAPTER 4

MAGGIE

Still Tuesday, Still in the Hospital

Maggie's grandchildren take to the hall, and red-eyed Clair shuts the door. She hooks Roger's arm. They advance, the two of them buttoned to the collar in overcoats, Roger in funereal-black, Clair in Ann Taylor blue. Their determined strides eat away the space from door to bed.

Maggie slips into the bed, covers pulled to her chin. She misses Hank. He'd derail the attack. And Jeremy. She misses him, too. He had a way of mellowing everyone, a calmer head when the tops of others came unscrewed. He's gone, and Maggie sees her son's screws loosening. *Pressing his white collar won't help.*

Denial, such a waste when a warm touch might heal. Why not let himself feast on Jeremy?

And Roger thinks I have a screw loose.

Tenderness. She wants it for the boys. She wants it for Clair, too, that bliss felt across a room, across miles, even years like she'd had with their father—long dead Dan.

Roger offers it to every supplicant at Curry House, the beloved homeless at his charity workplace. *At least he's not like Clair, trying to take over.*

Maggie works at understanding. *Clair can't manage her own life; why mess with mine?*

And here they come with no cheer, no desire to perk up the sick. *Why should they? I'm not sick. Not anymore.*

The silent monitors declare Maggie fit as a fiddle. No tape holds a needle in her vein, though she takes the occasional pill. Her body works.

She walks fine since replacing hospital slippers with Dear Dan's wingtips. And what a struggle that was, asking Clair to bring them. *I can fly in wingtips.* But no, "They're too big," she said. *Thank heaven for Rog.*

Now it's merely red tape holding her. So many hoops, and she's tired of jumping. Insurance this. Social worker that. A load of legalese. It's all positively mummifying.

Outside the window, a shadow passes. Cutting the sun, it's gone too fast for old eyes. She collects birds, her life list long and lost, yet the passion persists. Her favorite, the ring-necked pheasant, all copper and gold iridescence, red face, a white necklace. They burst from the underbrush…

Confusion sucks her into its vortex and leaves Maggie a living Witch of the East withering under a house.

"Mum?" Clair calls, her voice a far-off summons.

In bed, Maggie continues roaming the sky till her hands relax on her chest. The crushing house lifts inch by inch.

"She's not with us," Clair says.

"A momentary lapse," Roger whispers. "Let's do it later."

"There is no later."

"Gently, then," Roger says. "Her heart."

Clair strips off her coat and lays it on the end of the bed. She tightens the belt on her slacks and takes a deep breath. "Mum." Her voice has a layer of gentle concern over *something*, making Maggie suspicious.

Returning, Maggie laces her fingers. The band cuffed to her wrist reminds her she's a captive. She averts her face.

A little louder, Clair says, "Mum, listen."

Her head snaps around. "You sound like my mother." Maggie glowers at Clair. "You're the child here, not me."

"It's important." Roger grinds his foot on the floor as if squashing a roach.

"Go," says Maggie. "Boss your homeless people around."

"I don't have to; *they* pay attention."

"Getting testy, Rog?"

෨ ෫

Roger's been edgy since Clair got firm: "My futon's off limits." A reasonable method of pushing him toward Jeremy. *Too bad it backfired.* Now he's living at Curry House full time. *He's taken hiding too far.*

ဢ G

"Mum," Roger examines his fingernails. "Tomorrow, you'll be discharged."

"And..." Clair waves an encouraging hand.

Roger smiles. Brittle. Breakable. "We've found you a home."

Clair shakes her head and rams her hands deep in her pockets.

Busy absorbing cracks in Roger's face, Maggie can't translate words into meaning. She writes laboriously on the blackboard in her mind: "Found You A Home." Wrinkles in her forehead deepen. "Found?" She narrows her eyes. "I have a home."

"We've figured it out," Clair says, cajoling like Roger. "You'll be with me," she says, biting her lip. "For now, so you won't be lonely."

Maggie's chest constricts. *Liar, liar.* She waits for Clair's pants to ignite. "It's a nice offer," she says trying to sound grateful. It's hard to be grateful for a one-way ticket to Bedlam. Or was Bedlam a stopover, making The Home look like heaven instead of a life-stifling hall of terminal boredom.

Either way, thoughts of Clair's Grand Central house kick at Maggie.

"I won't be lonely." Her voice climbs. "Not with Clyde."

"You need more than a cat," says Clair.

"Being away from home, that's what makes me lonely." She misses the fire glowing behind andirons, misses her dinner companions—respectful ancestors confined in gold frames. They don't ask what she ate for breakfast or comment on her evening martini. Five olives were never a bone of contention.

ဢ G

The day she moved to Cambridge, a pheasant flew across her yard, and she knew she'd found the right home, a messenger from childhood: *You'll be happy here.* Big windows felt like she owned the sky, yet the living room was cozy, with floor-to-ceiling bookshelves, a red and blue Oriental in front of a sofa, the sofa good for Hank's several overnight visits, and her wingchair by the fireplace. A smaller rug at the side of her canopied bed warmed her feet, *Gatsby* on the bedside table—home.

The Great Gatsby. Reading it for the third time, she felt for him, his hopeless grasping at what he'd lost. Maggie looked for a different outcome every time she came to the end.

Until now, she'd basked in the glow of the fire, Dvorak filling the room, at peace under the benevolent eye of family portraits and the Hudson River flowing in its gold frame. She wallowed in the chair, Clyde curled in her lap, and talked to the potted plants. Her cat, her plants, and her paintings—all the friends she needed. *When they talk back, then I'll know I'm crazy.*

She won't give up her home. It's taken years to escape how she *should* live, struggling against Mother, her husband, neighbors, friends, and too often herself, all with truckloads of expectation.

For twenty years she's been in her own home, so hard-won, a place she truly fits.

⃝⃠

Maggie balls the sheet in a fist by her leg. "Clair," she says. "It's kind of you." But Clair's house is a wreck. Money is tight. *She doesn't need another complication.* "I'm better off at home."

Clair pinches the bridge of her nose. "Oh Mum, you can't be alone."

"I'm seventy-nine, old enough to do as I please."

"It's not that you're too old to…" *The lie bright in her eyes.*

"How did I get from 'too young' to 'too old,' no passing Go, no collecting two hundred dollars, not even a Get Out of Jail free card?"

"We just want..." Roger reaches a placating hand, "...want you to be happy."

"And safe." Clair circles an arm around Roger's waist. *Locked in a phalanx. The phalanx, that's how Ancient Greeks crushed their enemies. All these two need is a spear and a pike.*

"I'll be happier in Cambridge," she says. "I'll be safe."

Clair, low and gravely, "Jesus, Rog, spell it out." Then at Maggie, "Nooo, Mum, you need care."

A keeper, she means. A jailer.

Clair has told Maggie what to do and what not to do, so many forbidden things, how can Maggie keep order? She hadn't done that to them as kids. No, she reasoned with them.

Against the odds, Roger had been a cooperative teen, kind as Dr. Jekyll, and now look at him, a regular Mr. Hide. She grins at her own joke. *It's nothing to joke about.*

"You'll have a room to yourself." Clair—sweet, cajoling. Chirpy Clair. Irritating.

Now wait a minute. What room?

At Clair's house, the extra bed sat in the hall alcove. The one Roger tried to commandeer. The same place Maggie once slept for visits, a place smaller than her cell in boarding school. She swallows hard.

⅒⅓

Before Maggie's first hospital stay, she'd been at Clair's for several days to attend Trumpet-Girl's recital, and Hockey-Boy's varsity game.

Usually Maggie didn't stay over, but with evening events it seemed easier. Or so Clair had said. "You can have my room."

Once Maggie had done that, out of necessity, but taking her bed never felt right.

"Don't be silly." Maggie wouldn't have it. "It's only a few nights." Clair needed her rest. Maggie could catch up when she went home.

The first night in the second-floor alcove didn't bode well for those to follow, the space jammed with its keyhole desk, a stool beneath, and a questionable couch. Maggie helped Clair unfold the thing. "It's a futon," Clair always claimed, sounding the same way she did when passing off tofu as beef.

The mattress, when out flat, blocked the desk and stretched into the hall. Clair made the bed, and Maggie knelt on it, rummaging in her suitcase open on the desktop. She extracted her nightgown and kit, wobbled off the mattress, and headed to the bathroom they all shared.

She wanted to put her kit on the sink, but thought better of it. That one bathroom, everyone in the house used it. *What a minefield. And Rog wants to live here? I'd never.*

As Maggie approached the door, she heard quacking. *As in, duck.*

Inside, mist clung to the mirror. She kicked a wet towel into a corner and propped her kit on a stepstool. No place to hang her nightgown, she laid it over the edge of the tub, careful not to let it slip into the swamp of gray water where dinosaurs munched on camouflage-colored boats. A shark lay beached on a washcloth, a Barbie's leg in its mouth. Opposite the tub, the toilet gleamed, the seat up. Inside the porcelain oasis, a yellow ducky swam. Quack-quacking, it circled the bowl.

Maggie brushed her teeth and washed her face. She had to have a discussion with the duck. Since he wouldn't quit swimming, she plucked him out, webbed feet gyrating, and set him in the swampy tub. As if offended, the duck beached himself in Barbie's hair and gave a last dispirited quack.

Returning to the alcove, Maggie folded her clothes into the suitcase-turned-bureau before lowering herself stiffly onto the futon. She clicked off the light, and let sleep take her, "sleep" being a generous term for the night's activity.

First, Clair marched up and down the hall on restless legs. She did it on tiptoes, but her feet, so close to Maggie's head in passing, were hard to ignore.

Hank came next, the best part of not sleeping, he in his footy PJs, cape, and mask. He did a quick-step pee-dance. "Gotta go, back in a minute."

True to his word, he returned, his sleeve damp. From washing his hands? *I hope so.*

"Someone moved my duck." Hank sat on the side of her futon, legs crossed on the floor. "Nana, do you think, if I pulled my tongue really, really hard, I could turn myself inside out?"

"Might hurt," she said.

"Mmmm, you know what hurts?" He pushed the sleeve past his wrist. "I went down the giant slide, headfirst!"

"Is that allowed?"

"Celeste said, Zip can't go to heaven, Mrs. Mouse neither." He wiped his nose on his dry sleeve. "I said, if they can't, she can't. She pulled my hair."

Maggie leaned on one elbow. "No escape, I take it?"

"I got the naughty chair."

Clair's door opened. "Hank, get to bed."

"You better," Maggie said. "Or we'll both get the naughty chair."

"I wish you lived here, Nana."

Living with Hank could be fun, but this house? *Oh, Lordy.*

For a few hours, quiet descended, except for the squeak of an exercise wheel as one of Hank's seven mice ran to nowhere. Then, her least favorite visitor.

Groans came from Hockey-Boy's room. A wet dream? His door opened and slammed. Then, with the clicking of four sets of toenails, Zip came down from the third floor. The wire-haired hound sniffed his way to the alcove and lovingly slurped his wet beard across Maggie's face. She shoved him and rolled over. Undaunted, he stretched out beside her, his back against hers. He made little squeaking noises, and a suffocating stench filled the air. His flatulent mishaps made hers seem minor.

⁞⁞

Maggie sits straighter in the hospital bed. "I'm not going," she says. "Not to your house."

"You'll like it, Mum. We're putting a new bath..." When Clair lies, her cheek twitches up by the left eye. *Like now.*

"It's for the best." Clair squares her shoulders. "Your place, we had to..." Roger jabs an elbow in her side.

Clair drops her arm from around him. Nose to his nose, she says in an angry whisper, "She's got to know."

"Know what?" Maggie asks. She swings boney feet over the bedside and plants them cold on the floor, her legs long and bare below the johnny.

"We sold it," Clair says. She jerks her head at Rog as if to say, "There, it's done."

Maggie blinks "My home?" She wipes spittle from the corner of her mouth. Her eyebrows crimp in confusion. She rubs aching knees.

"We close in a few days." Clair lets out a long breath.

Maggie rocks on the bedside. If Clyde purred in her lap, she'd stroke him, and the tightness in her chest would ease.

"Clyde!" Maggie sets her fingernails in the mattress. "What have you done with Clyde?"

CHAPTER 5

CLAIR

A Never-Ending Guilt

Doing this to Mum, it's worse than caging an exotic bird.
Clair had seen it first hand as a kid. Her friend Susie, all excited
over her gift of a Rainbow Lorikeet fresh from the forests of
Australia, a bright creature bedecked in blue, green, red, yellow,
and orange. The bird flung itself at the bars until exhausted,
then sat bewildered on the cage floor. Only a few months later,
the colors dulled and the feathers dropped. Clair wouldn't visit
there, even after the bird died.

Mum being at Clair's house after the original operation didn't
seem like caging. That was temporary, granted a long temporary,
but this time, it would be permanent.

Back then, Mum had admired her surgeon. At her first
appointment she'd whispered, "Clair, did you see his hands?
Artist's hands!" An artist herself, clearly Mum itched for her
pencil and pad, wanting to draw his hands. Clair could see the
aura of their magical talent in her mother's eyes.

Mum had magic fingers, the way she could capture the likeness
of people in three strokes. She was an acclaimed portrait painter
who volunteered for her church fair, making quick sketches of
people lined up around the tent.

Her serious portraits took months, the results intense, as if
the person awaited their turn to speak, their essence palpable.
She painted Father in his last months, warmth in the creases
around his eyes, his defenseless bald head, love in every stroke
of the brush.

When she surfaced from her grief, museums and books whet
Mum's appetite for crawling through caves, Ajanta to Lascaux.
She strolled through churches and down into bone-filled

catacombs, then took to the sky in a glider, determined to see her solo world from every angle.

Weeks after surgery the gauze helmet came off. Half her head had been shaved and now, still in the hospital, hair grew from fuzz to coarse gray spikes.

"When there's a roadblock, the brain makes new pathways," the surgeon assured them. Clair imagined bulldozers and backhoes, trucks of hot-top paving the way to Mum's recovery.

Clair fed her lunch from a divided dish, spoonful by spoonful: applesauce, liquid oatmeal, milk from a cup. Later, like a toddler, she struggled with the spoon, and wore her meals across her face.

English words began to form with little glimpses of meaning, and a month later Clair took her home to Lexington—a banner day, the yard wild with tulips and daffodils. Clair wheeled her over the threshold into the hall. Roger kept a hand on her shoulder while the kids brought in her suitcase and vases of bright snapdragons. She held fast to her small satchel, the book she'd taken unread, pencil leads broken, blank paper crushed.

From the wheelchair, she peered through the wide doorway into Clair's front room, probing every shelf and corner. Her eyes widened with panic, the same look she'd had years before when thieves had emptied her house.

The first month at home, Clair bathed her as they'd done in the hospital. She wiped her mother's wrinkled brow with a washcloth, ran it down the cords of her neck, under collapsed breasts and over her laddered ribs, washing and rinsing the loose skin.

Those months with Mum, Clair came to know her body better than any mother would want her child to know.

Over a year, and Mum outgrew her infancy. She learned to walk wielding two canes, eventually no cane, and worked her way to a determined independence.

But regression has taken hold and Clair sees catastrophe ahead, yet it feels like a fine line between safety and incarceration. Renovations at home will help, but Clair hates having her hand on the cage door.

CHAPTER 6

HANK

Tuesday, Late Afternoon

Nana's Cambridge kitchen. Major Amazing Man, mask on, squats on a stool at the counter. Part raptor, he hulks over a pad of paper. He tips onto his toes. Elbows on the counter. Knees to his chin. Blue cape across his shoulders. A fat black pencil in his fist, he fills a dinosaur's mouth with teeth.

Uncle Rog opens Nana's cabinet. "What do we do with clay stuff?" He holds a monster by the neck.

"Chuck them all." Ma doesn't even look.

"I made those." Hank jumps off the stool. "I..." with his fists, he bangs the lightning bolt on his chest. "I gave them to Nana." Two hands on Uncle R's belt, Hank shoves him from the cabinet, slams the door with his elbow.

Ma groans. "This has to be done *now.*" She folds a box shut. "The movers..." she looks at her watch. "Three hours, that's all we have."

Feet apart, Hank puts his back to the cabinet. "Nana's gonna be pissed."

"Don't use that word."

He spreads his arms, blocking the door. "You're wrecking everything." He growls. He bares his teeth.

Ma and Uncle R shift to the bedroom. Hank follows. He watches them pull blankets off the mattress. Sheets too. They tip the mattress against the wall. Unscrew the bed ends.

"Where's she going to sleep?"

Ma nudges him with her hip. "Off the rug." She rolls it into a giant Tootsie Roll.

"You're being bad." Hank kneels by a half-full box. He empties Nana's collection of hammers, oil cans, strange scissors, a horseshoe. "She loves these."

"Please," Ma says. "Stop. I don't have time for this." She turns her back and blows her nose.

Uncle R lifts Hank and, back in the kitchen, sets him on the counter. "You know she's moving. Now finish your picture. Here, use color." Uncle R takes pens from Nana's drawer. "Give it to Nana."

"When?"

"When she's settled," Ma says.

He shuffles the colored pens. "Dino-mo eats bad people." He chooses a green pen, the same green as the blaze on his shirt. His face close to the paper, he pushes the mask to the top of his head, draws the dinosaur's hind legs, adds little arms, the fingers with claws.

He sniffs. Mmmm, a smelly marker, the forever kind. No washing off. He caps it and stuffs it in his pants pocket. Ma can't know.

"How big is a dinosaur brain?" he asks. Ma isn't listening.

He draws a pea-sized circle. Got to be smarter than that.

"What about her dishes?" Uncle R stacks plates on the table, the ones with pictures of fruit in the middle. "They're valuable. We could sell them on eBay."

"Be my guest," says Ma.

"As if I had time." He wraps the stack in newspaper.

"You think I do?"

"And these creepy things?" He holds up Nana's candlesticks.

Hank bangs a marker on his picture. "She needs them." He draws a raptor tattoo on his arm. Mouth open. More teeth.

Uncle R forces a box shut. "Odds are she'll..."

"Shhh." Ma raises a hand. She leans her head toward Hank.

Hank gives the Dino-tattoo boney fingers to his fingernails. He goes back to the paper. "Everything's odd." Dinosaur breath blows a cyclone, whirling hair on a stick figure. Hank whispers to the figure, "Run, Nana, run."

He draws a bubble at her mouth: HELP. Help. Where *are* you Major Amazing Man? He can't spell Amazing, and besides, all that won't fit in the bubble.

Ma takes the last picture off the wall. "No room for this." She adds it to the stack by the door. "I wish…"

"I wish we hadn't sold," Uncle R says.

"But we did, and the closing's day after tomorrow." Ma kicks a box. "Oh, shoot, Friday's Hank's half day."

"He can't go to court." Uncle R keeps packing.

"He'll stay in Gill's office."

Uncle R drops a plate. It smashes. "GILL?" He looks like he'll puke. "Our old neighbor?"

"I meant Gilbert, Mum's guy." She tapes another box. "But why not Gill? He's a lawyer."

"He's a…"

"A what?"

Uncle R knocks a stack of books off the table. "Tell you later."

No one says anything. Ma stuffs more things into garbage bags. Uncle R picks up the books, packs them, and kicks the cat carrier. "What about this?"

"A spare, the good one's at home." Ma covers her eyes. "I wish Clyde was."

"What?" says Uncle R.

"The plumber let him out."

"Don't worry, he'll be back when he's hungry." Uncle R slides the carrier into the out pile. "At least the bathroom's finished."

"But Clyde's a lap cat. And he doesn't know our neighborhood," Ma says.

"He's Mum's cat; he's a survivor."

Ma makes a gargley noise. Uncle R stops packing. He hugs her. They keep standing there till Ma shakes loose. "Hank," she says. "Help pack the car."

"Somerville Goodwill?" Uncle Rog rubs Ma's back. "I'll drive."

"Too much stuff. Boston's better."

"It'll take days." Uncle R pushes a full bag through the front door. "I already feel like Hank's mouse running in its wheel."

"Ma." Hank off his stool again. "You know how Mrs. Mouse got out?"

"You *let* her out."

"Yeah, well...she came back all fat." Hank walks in a circle. "When Nana's back, will she have little Nanas?" He looks up.

Uncle R covers his mouth. "It's time you two had a...*chat.*"

"I'll drive." Ma pulls out keys. "Hank, you stay with Uncle Rog. Keep packing; and Rog, feel free to have that chat."

Seven mice drive Ma crazy. What would she do with seven Nanas?

CHAPTER 7

MAGGIE

Wednesday

Out of bed, Maggie sits in a chair, tray-table pressed to her belly. Two fried eggs quiver on her plate. She stabs a yolk with her fork, and yellow slithers into the triangled toast.

She slogs through what she heard yesterday; *something important, what?* It's on the tip of her.... *nose, doze... Close...* "Closing!"

Clair bumps through the door, her arms loaded. Maggie's thoughts splinter.

Clair blows stray hair from her eyes. "Hank, get in here. You're worse than Zip."

Clair's flatulent hydrant-sniffer.

In one hand Clair carries a garment bag; in the other, an aged train-case, square and hard with a handle on top. "Time to go," she says. "Let's get you dressed."

Hank teeters around the room on his heels and then on his toes in a castoff pair of Trumpet-Girl's red Mary-Janes. Arms above his head, one hand chases the other, thumb and pinky out as if flying. The chaser-hand nips at the chased, banks, and cuts back to bite the other's tail.

"You need a leash." Clair angles him to a chair. "Sit." Fanning her face, she unbuttons her blue coat, the mismatched plaids of her skirt and jacket exposed. *She must really be harried.*

Hank plops in the chair, legs straight, head back, and with a click of his heels the chase continues, hands roaming above his head. A running dialogue follows the action, Hank narrating in two voices, the words not quite audible.

Maggie points at the train-case. "That's not mine."

"No? It was in your closet." Clair opens it. "Damn." She slams the lid.

Great! And she's taking charge?

Maggie pokes the zippered bag now lying on the bed. "And this? This is dress up."

Clair scowls.

Hank shrugs. "You said bring Nana a coat. It's Grizzly, her favorite."

Hank loves it, too. His right-hand bites the left and wrestles it to his lap.

"Stop that." Then under her breath, Clair says, "An hour..." She ticks off on her fingers, "...home, a dress, meet the bus. Oh God, Zip's at the vet." She heads for the door. "I should be back in... Ack, your pills... two hours? Three?" She pushes Hank. "Up," she says.

He holds onto the door handle. "I'll stay with Nana."

"Not a chance, Bub."

From her chair, Maggie watches the door swing without closing completely.

Closing! It doesn't mean closed.

Fidgeting by the bed, Maggie looks for her watch. *Two, three hours.* She can feel Clair, in the form of Elvira Gulch, bearing down with a bag she'll throw over Maggie's head.

I need... what's he called...a hair-splitter, a glitz spinner. She plunges through oniony layers of the past. She had a guy once, a helper guy. *What's he called, a word wizard.*

Maggie remembers a tower with rabbit-run hallways, offices and offices, and his on the corner. She can see his big windows overlooking trees, a pond in the distance, the city mixed with country.

A ridiculous vision? She shakes her head. *Better than horses through the wall.* She hunches her shoulders and waits.

"No, not a vision—the park," she crows.

The L-word, that's what he was. Yes. *Lawyer lawyer, overlooking Boston's big park.* Repetition pins the word like a Post-it in her head. At home, she had yellow stickies, plus a pen on every table. The stickies kept her on track.

She'll sic her lawyer on them. *A foot in the door—no closing.*

Maggie pulls on heavy socks, *Bless Rog,* and jams her feet into Dan's roomy wingtips. *I'll fly right out of here.*

She opens the case. *Mother's case, not mine.* Inside a jumble of white-capped vials waits. Maggie squints at the names: Klonopin, Lasix, Xanax, Triazolam. *Waste not, want not.*

Is that what Maggie thought way back when she saved them? Repurpose the pills?

Clair had removed all medications, even aspirin from Maggie's bathroom cabinet.

Morning, noon, and night in the hospital, if a pill was needed, a nurse stood over Maggie. It's well past noon. *Should I take one now? Two? They'd been good for Mother. Good for the goose, good for the gosling.*

She feels an earlier Post-it curl, the message unreadable. *As important as pills?*

More so.

Think.

She digs underneath the vials, sifts through a hairbrush, lipstick, curlers, nail clippers, a compact, eye shadow, a pocketknife, and at the bottom, her mother's pearl-handled pistol nestles in a stack of monogramed handkerchiefs. *Mother never traveled without her protective friend.* And perfume. Chanel rises, resurrecting Mother right here in the hospital. *You're going out like that? Put on your face, Maggie.*

Make-up never seemed worth the time. Her face was her face and taking the shine off her nose wouldn't make it less sharp, and certainly no prettier. *I tried, honest.* But she'd chew the lipstick off before she left the house. By the end of an evening, eye shadow drifted to her temples. Mascara ran rivulets down her cheeks. Not the look Mother sought.

Maggie unzips the bag stretched on the bed, plump as an occupied body bag. She parts the opening and lifts the corpses of sixty mink sewn seamlessly together. Silky smooth, and the victim of only a bit of mothy corruption. *I hate moths. Nibble-nibble in the dark.* She blows at the dusty destruction and slides her cheek against the fur.

୨୦ଔଓ

Hank loved sloshing around in that coat. On visits to her house, he made a great grizzly, and she became Grizzly Adams chasing him until he turned on her. Then, she tamed him with ice cream.

୨୦ଔଓ

Maggie slides her arms through the silk-lined sleeves, cool on bare skin. The coat covers her brown spotted legs and goes over the red topped hunting socks down to her wingtips. *Hurry, Maggs.*

Lawyer, lawyer. She smooths the yellow sticky flat in her mind. *An address would help.*

She searches the coat pockets and finds nothing, but in the secret pocket she feels the stash of her mother's ever present mad money, two Lincolns wrapping a Liberty silver dollar.

A quick swipe of the brush through gray hair and Maggie pins the twist away from her face. She nods to Mother in the mirror. *Ready.*

Maggie checks her wrist, no watch, only the white hospital shackle sliding on her narrow bones. Maggie feels five again, as if making off with a slab of pecan pie warm from the windowsill. If caught, Father would've tanned her hide. *Clair might do worse.*

She strides for the door. The mink falls open, exposing her striped johnny. *Ack.* She clutches it shut, her motion too desperate not to be noticed. When sneaking out, the sneaker can't look sneaky.

A belt. Her eyes comb the bed, rumpled sheets falling to the floor, the tray table piled with Styrofoam cups, a blood pressure cuff, a phone. The only cord she sees belongs to the phone. She stretches the black spiral, both arms extended wide, and whips its plug from the socket. Winding the cord around her middle, she nestles a line in the fur, the flat phone a pendant hanging at her side.

The body bag lies on the bed, and best of all, she's not in it. If she were, at least Maggie's death would save Clair from her overweening sense of responsibility.

Take the case. No, just the pills and penknife. And the pistol? Why not, Mother would.

Pockets full, down the hall, she passes open rooms where TVs blare bombings, the images of dismemberment too grim to erase. With all the things she wants to remember and can't, why retain dismemberment?

৪০ ০৪

Bombs. Brother Bobby made them. Encouraged by a chemistry set for his birthday, he invented concoctions in test tubes. Heated over a Bunsen burner, to his delight the results foamed over his bureau, corroding his penknife and ruining seven scout badges.

As he got older, the chemistry became more focused. With the final set, age twelve to Maggie's eight, he made gunpowder.

"Let's test it," he said.

৪০ ০৪

Too bad. *Where's Bobby now?* She'd like to explode the hospital.

Militant in mink, spine straight, collar up, she marches toward the nurses' station. She keeps her head turned from the nurse manning the desk. *How does a woman man a desk?*

"May I help you?" The woman keeps her eyes on her work.

Maggie in rabbity-panic: "I'm late, I'm late, for a very important—" *Get a grip, this isn't Wonderland.*

Head high, she marches sedately toward the elevator. She punches the down button. Ding. And flowing with the others, she crams into the box, a white-coated doctor sandwiched beside her.

Floor six, floor five. He looks at the hospital tag on her wrist. *Shit.*

She never used to say "shit." She should have snipped the band and left it on the bedside table. Hiking her elbow inside the sleeve, she eases down the cuff. *That's it, slowly now. Doctors smell fear.*

The air in the elevator thickens with perfumes and soaps cloying together. Floor four, floor three. Two. One. The doors slide open.

She sweeps out with the crowd as a waft of cold caresses her face. The hospital lobby spreads before her, doors rotating an invitation to blue sky. *Hank loves revolving doors.* She shuffles into the pie-shaped opening and pushes the door. She'd like to go around twice in Hank's honor, but the door shoots her out onto the sidewalk.

She takes the slope between parking garages, other women beside her, their heels clicking cement. A siren deafens. Cringing, hands tight to her ears, she squinches her eyes. An ambulance whooshes past, and she hums to herself, heart thrumming till the wailing stops.

Her eyes pop open and catch a shadow passing overhead. It disappears behind buildings, reappears over traffic on the cross street, and veers up Beacon Hill. *A pheasant?*

On the farm, she lured them—in their glory, all wary and wild—out of the hedgerow brush and into the yard. All it took was a scatter of dry corn.

Going to the Public Garden, I bet? She follows alongside Cambridge Street traffic and strikes uphill on the narrow sidewalk. As she picks her way past cellar stairs inviting a tumble, her legs complain. A bothersome bumping hits low at her hem. *The pistol. Must be a hole in the pocket.*

Winded, she takes Revere, the street downhill toward distant cars whizzing along Storrow, then left on Charles with its multiple antique boutiques—*and oh hell, is that Clair?* Wearing the same blue coat, a woman comes out of the drugstore.

Maggie backs up to a door marked antiques and pushes with her rump. A bell above her head jangles. *Good god, tell the world why don't you.* She waits by the door, her spine pressed to the wall.

The saleswoman approaches, her eyes registering the mink, *Cha-ching, cha-ching. When people see mink, nothing else matters.*

"Are you looking for something specific?" asks the woman.

No, something specific is looking for me. "Just browsing, thanks." It's hard to browse and hide at the same time.

Maggie pokes her head around the door. No blue coat. "Gotta run." And she bolts.

Block after block, she hustles toward tall trees in the distance. *Ah, almost there.*

Threading around the Garden's corner gate, she tips her head to the sky. *Freedom! Uplifting as a Beefeater martini.*

A butterfly of excitement beats in her chest. *This is excitement, right?*

Maggie had always turned fear into excitement for the kids when lightning struck. They'd all scrunch into a pig-pile with the dog on Maggie's bed. The house shuddered, but so what?

Now the kids don't soothe so easily, even in daylight. They look at Maggie with suspicion, as if she might take off her clothes in the middle of a restaurant.

Maggie peers down at a snippet of johnny. For a second, the fuzzy moth of fright tickles her ribs. The beating wings, similar to the butterflies—*Beware the evil flipside*—so like laughter. How it climbs and climbs and at its peak, tears threaten to snatch her, tumble her ass over teakettle into the doldrums.

No, the johnny doesn't count; I'd never strip naked.

She steps a gingery dance along the asphalt path, coattails bouncing. The pills in her pocket rattle a maraca rhythm.

To her delight, the Garden rolls green, the trees her friends, so like the farm where she lived as a kid.

ಹಿ ಅ

That farm mellows her insides, always there whole and unchanged. She sees the fieldstone house, how it stood at the center of lush green acres with hedgerows dividing fields full of sheep and horses. An orchard flowered, the trees promising baskets of apples, peaches, and plums.

Her red, hay-filled barn breathed with geese, a sow raising shoats, a pair of Japanese silkies decked out in white flowing feathers. The rooster's predawn warble raised the sun, spilling brilliance through bedroom windows.

On that farm, Maggie stayed nested warm in the family bosom, the seasons flowing in seamless renewal. But her father's death changed the world. Assets flash-frozen, Mother sold their home, and life as they knew it ceased.

Maggie won't let it happen again.

Not this time.

Without the farm, the sun seemed to sleep, Maggie groping at the dark until her stepfather opened a whole new existence. Maggie wasn't Cinderella, so nothing wicked came her way. He provided meat at every meal, petticoats, dresses, alligator shoes and a bag to match, a beaver coat for her, a mink for her mother. Yet, this wasn't home.

Spoiled child. Lying in a four-poster, she missed her rope-tied bed, peepers singing arias, the smell of hay she'd mown herself. Boots, dungarees, the sweet stink of manure.

୫୬ ୯୬

As she did then, she wants her own home, not just someone taking her in with a pat on the head, and a "There, there, dear, everything's fine." *It won't be fine unless I... I what...*

PART III

ON THE LOOSE

CHAPTER 8

MAGGIE

Wednesday Afternoon

But yes, here in the Garden, everything *is* fine. If only the mothy tickle in her chest would quit.

Tickle, schmickle, work through it.

Work, her universal antidote. And see, the sun smiles, a fine time for camping. She'll bed on pine boughs tonight, the same way she did on the farm with Bobby.

Dear dead Bobby. Her brother had been killed by a drunk driver the month he returned from Vietnam. She carries him with her, his ready advice at hand.

They camped hundreds of times in the woods. She and Bobby set traps. Oh, the thrill of the catch, the skinning, the roasting, the rich aroma of browning meat. She did it then, of course, she'll do it today. Except Peter—

Peter Rabbit that is. She read him to Clair and Rog and, more recently, Hank. Now the thought of Peter's little blue jacket abandoned beside her campfire makes her weep.

Never mind, she'll figure out something. There's more than one way to snare lunch.

She dances further into the Garden and, "Oh, ducks," yells Maggie. There they are, a bronze line waddling on rows of cobbles.

Her wingtips slalom through the shiny-headed ducklings. "Hi Jack," she says, and with a hand to each head, "Hi Mack, hi Pack, hi Nack, hi Quack." She lacks the other names, but keeps dancing. *Too bad Hank isn't here, he'd ride Mrs. Mallard.*

As if channeling her thoughts, a boy with a willow switch, a boy too big for such shenanigans, swings his leg over Mrs. Mallard. "This is how you ride a duck," he says to his friend, and knees up by his ears, he settles his rump on Mrs. Mallard's

45

back. "Giddy-ap," he cries, and thrashes her drumstick with the switch.

"Give it to her good." The other hooligan laughs. He rocks on the heels of his untied high-tops and holds his stomach.

"Young man." Maggie marches at them, past Mack, Pack, and Quack. "Stop that."

Over his shoulder, the rider gives her a snot-nosed leer. "Says who?"

"Says me," says she swinging the phone cord. The handset whistles with each rotation as she closes on them.

"Jesus, lady." The rider leapfrogs over Mrs. Mallard's head. "It's not a real duck." His friend doubles over. In hysterics, they slap each other and run.

Seething, she stands guard, phone ready, until the boys hoot their way across the leaf-covered grass, under the willows, and out of sight.

Finally calm, Maggie ambles on down the asphalt path, eyeing the old Hancock's cupola. It shines blue, its weather light on top, a match to the bright sky.

Gulls circle overhead calling her, while puffs of Indian summer fill her with joy. She spreads her arms to the late afternoon, her mink open wing-and-wing, the johnny luffing. Under full sail, running before the wind, she tips her arms and turns, wheeling the way gulls do.

Once more into the blow, the mink slaps her body. The fickle breeze nips her legs.

She shivers. Silk in the lining of her mink magnifies the cold. *It's not fair (I sound like Hockey-Boy)*, a fur coat should be warm. *Count your blessings, it's not raining.*

She snuggles close into the collar. Too bad the whole thing isn't lined with mink. The wind picks up, icing the silk. Breezy fingers slip under her johnny and give her a goose. Her heart jumps. She stamps her foot. If that wind had a face, she'd slap it.

You want a fur-lined coat? Use your brain.

She ducks behind a bush, takes a deep breath, and strips off the mink. Her johnny blows up to her armpits, exposing deep wrinkled thighs. The wind hoots.

She squawks and fights the high-side of her flying johnny, clamping it with an elbow. Then the other side blows up. *Oh Hell.*

Giving up on the johnny, she rams a fast arm in one sleeve of the mink, grips the cuff, pulls, and one sleeve done, she turns the other. The outside now silky as a chrysalis, she worms into the fur-lined sleeves, the front overlapped and belted tight, the curly cord dark on light brown silk. The handle of the phone cord dangles.

Fur so friendly and warm on her skin, she hugs the coat. "That's better," she says and leaves the bush behind.

The cord tied tight, she launches herself again and cruises around the mulch-covered beds, where tulips sleep for the winter. Poor flowers, tight bulbs trapped in formal beds. Surely, they'd rather be free in the fields.

She wants to dig them up. *But watch it, Maggs!* By the pond, blue-uniformed men sniff the path. They scan the water, now devoid of swans. Some busybody bureaucrats had locked them away. They promised, just for the winter. *Clair will lock me up forever.*

Maggie sidles next to a willow, keeping it between herself and the uniforms. Then, on stealthy toes, slips from willow to pine to beech, the trees shielding her as they did in the woods, Maggie an Indian to brother Bobby's cowboy. *No forced reservation for this brave.*

Coming closer, her would-be captors swing clubs. Their laughter barks as their heels thud against the path, closer with every step.

Behind the beech, rigid as the tree, she shifts her feet inch-by-inch, breath held. She waits as they eye the thinning stream of passers-by.

Finally, the men move on through the gate and, breath out, she kisses the tree as clouds build overhead and the chill increases. Smoochers under a reddened maple draw a blanket around their bodies. Really? Could they think the blanket hides their groping? Or is the couple flaunting what they see as their exclusive right, sex the prerogative of the young? Wouldn't they be surprised to know it gets better with age; a secret the old hold close.

⋈

Maggie's grandmother had told her, but as a young woman, Maggie didn't believe—*Silly old soul what did she know?* So arrogant, the young always thinking they know best.

But she'd had fun back then, those first experimental touches, Dan and Maggie crowding his dorm-room bed, Dan slipping his hand under her shirt, his fingers soft, hesitant, advancing, retreating, almost kittenish in a quick skirmish under lace. Her nipples leapt to attention. Encouraged, his hand wandered her thigh as he whispered persuasive words, fingers inching, inching until he teased at the edge of her panties.

She hated the "No, no, not now," knowing she mustn't, until the Holy Grail of marriage, Maggie nearly in tears from the wanting.

Maggie sighs. *Goodie-two-shoes always won out.* Was it the threat of accidental procreation, or was it Mother and the weight of her disappointment? Or neighborly accusations of slutish behavior? *All those old codes, how they shift and change and somehow stay the same—* Clair buttoned in suburban blue, Roger in a corset of his own design. *So hard to break them out.*

Maggie herself didn't dare alfresco lovemaking, not till years after she and dear departed Dan married. Even then, or now for that matter, she wouldn't consider a public park in her own hometown, *For Lord's sake.*

Maybe the couple in the blanket, their breath coming faster and faster, the side-by-side position abandoned to missionary, his rear in the air and plunging; maybe they aren't from Boston.

All of this attention affects Maggie's nethers. She has to pee and glances around for a suitable place — after all, she's camping. Maybe the lovers are camping too.

Her need intensifies, and she skips behind the closest tree with a girth bigger than her own. She gathers furry coattails under her elbows and grasps a piece of johnny in each hand. No panties to pull. Apparently she's gone commando, as Hank would say. She'd prefer a pair of plain underwear, though commando means one less maneuver.

Ready? Hike.

A grinding of wheels sounds behind her. *Oh Hell.* She drops her tails, and swoosh, a skateboarder, close enough to touch, whoops, "Nice ass, Grannie." And off he zooms, long hair flying.

The Garden's not like the woods, where privacy waits behind any tree. Here, sadly, the trees come with another heavily peopled pathway.

She sees bigger trees and a green sign—Commonwealth Ave. These trees are perfect, with only one walkway between them and the way lit with streetlights, shadows behind every tree.

Approaching the fence, *Oh shoot,* Commonwealth won't do. Four lanes of traffic, headlights flashing, sandwich the trees. But beyond the fence, she spies the Ritz and…

And, *Oh God, oh God,* through the traffic noise a cloppety-cloppety bears down—*The Horsemen.*

Apocalyptic, The Four, how they haunt her. She squeezes her eyes shut, hands over her ears as the thunder of metal shodding approaches. She hears sparks on the asphalt path as each hoof hits. *Please not again.*

෧৩

It has happened before. At dinner one night with the whole family there, things got squiffy. She smelled burning toast. She felt drunk without the blessings of gin. Her lips trembled as her fingers clamped white on the edge of the table, and pain caught at her lungs.

"Nana." A whisper of giggles. "Is it horses again?"

Those horses, no lock kept them out. Too many to count, they burst through dining room walls, their hooves the size of restaurant plates. Legs thrashed as they vaulted over the heads of Maggie and the children. *So many children?*

Their dinners gobbled, her jokesters vied for cake, oblivious of fetlocks lashing their faces, oblivious of air heavy with heat and the smell of white-lathered sweat.

Cups chattered in their saucers; silverware clanged, and on came the horsemen—The Four, tall in their saddles. Horse-breath pinned Maggie to her chair.

"Hide," she whispered, "hide." And they, foolish tots, patted her hand, elbowed each other, and grinned.

⁎–⁐

Closer and closer, the cloppety comes through the dark. And *this time, they'll—*

She hunkers over her knees, head turtled, hands high, shielding her head. She waits.

But hey…hold on…

Head tilted, she listens. *Not four.* Not even two of the usual crowd. She un-crouches, rusty knees complaining.

Upright, the need to pee reasserts itself. She crosses her legs as one horse takes shape. It closes in, one horseman astride, no scythe. He's just a child wearing a green uniform, a badge, and flat-brimmed hat. He hauls on the reins, the horse skidding to a stop.

Her relief lasts less than a second. She'd rather The Four than this one blushing boy. *Damn, damn, double damn.* He's caught her. He'll arrest her, public urination at the very least, and *oh the headlines.* Clair will die of embarrassment. Roger will kill her, no horseman needed.

But I'm innocent. The act was incomplete. Surely intent isn't an arrestable offence.

"Ma'am." The fellow leans from his horse.

She retreats two steps from the hard-breathing animal, and clutches her coat at the neck.

"Are you alright? Did he hurt you?"

"Who?" Maggie takes another step back. The horse jigs. He snorts.

"The skateboarder, I saw him lift..." The rider chokes. "...your coat. I'll catch him." He wheels his horse and takes off. "You'll want to press charges," he calls from the dark. "Wait here."

"Wait?" *Not likely.*

A spit of rain increases her need, and Mother's favorite pit stop waits beyond the fence: The Ritz, though some prankster ruined the sign. Now it reads nonsense, T A J, not so much as a four-letter word. But she knows the Ritz when she sees it, the staid Back Bay brick, the welcoming door held open by a minion in black livery.

೮೦೮೪

After the farm, and Mother's remarriage, Mother had dragged teenaged Maggie inside the Ritz: Tat Sanders' for dresses. Firestone's for jewels, the final Newbury Street stop on their exhaustive search for suitable clothes. Then came the café, an oyster lunch plus a plate of sweets big enough to choke a horse—the lure to get Maggie shopping in the first place.

On top of all that, the Ritz was the most luxurious place to pee. Public restrooms gave Maggie the horrors, helped along by her mother's description of diseases available to her naked rump. Ringworm topped the list. Bursting was preferable, except at the Ritz.

೮೦೮೪

Knowing the desperation of Hank's pee-dance, she clamps her knees together and shuffles through an opening in the Garden's iron fence, and then crosses Arlington.

Dashing between raindrops, she confronts the Ritz entrance, only her collar showing the coat's mink. The doorman comes to attention. *What happened to him?*

No longer decked in black with a cap, he presents in red whiskers, a turban, pantaloons, and a sash with scimitar attached.

"Nice outfit," she says. "But Charles, you've changed." Mother always called him Charles.

His cheeks color, a match to his whiskers, but he stares straight ahead as if she doesn't exist. *Of all the…* She reaches for the door handle. He slides a half step and blocks her.

"Excuse me," she says, "I need to go in."

"I don't think so, madam." He looks past her head. "The Taj won't allow it."

"Who's this Taj?" Blood rises hot in her cheeks. Channeling her mother, she says, "He can't tell *me* what to do. I've always come to the Ritz."

"Madame, this is not the Ritz." He taps the sign by the door. "Taj Boston," he says. "The Ritz moved." He smiles for the first time. "Across the Common, I'm sure they'll be delighted to see you."

As Maggie turns to go, she catches a reflection in the dark window by the door: a wire-haired harridan in a frayed coat. *Those shoes, they're Dan's.*

She looks over her shoulder. No one's around except Charles. He watches her. She peers back at the reflection's face, so like Mother before she died, except for the wild hair and iffy outfit.

Her fingers waggle a greeting, and stricken by a surge of need, she stops. *Forget yourself, you'll wet your nonexistent nickers.* But across the common? She'll never make it.

She ducks around the corner to Newbury. No doorman watching that entrance. She turns her coat right side out and combs fingers through mats in her hair before re-twisting the strands.

Now believably Cambridge, she sails into the Taj, and hurries to the lobby. She knows where the 'Ladies' is, but... *Which where?* She circles in place.

A plump dowager sits in a straight-backed chair. She gives Maggie the fish-eye over the lip of her teacup, little finger extended. The saucer shakes in her other hand.

What a harpy. Maggie had seen those bedpost legs before. *A crone chaperone,* her ilk attending cotillion dances.

⁞⁞

Above the fray, those crones had glared from their balcony at gangly Maggie. She itched in her crinolines while boys, with glove-covered paws, stumbled in stiff new shoes. Noses at her throat, the silent fellows watched their feet, while she scanned the room clearly visible over the tops of their heads. One-two-three-, one-two-three, they clomped her raw-boned self around the floor.

⁞⁞

In her musings, Maggie trips over the dowager's cane protruding from under her thin-leg chair. The mink flaps open, disclosing a knee and a swath of blue stripes.

The dowager pulls in her chins. "Riffraff," she says to her cup. "The Ritz was never like this."

Maggie hurries to her left and down the stairs, the direction automatic. The clatter of the dowager's teacup returning to its saucer follows her.

Entering the pristine ladies' room, Maggie finds the only occupant a spray of vermillion orchids. The commodes hide demurely behind wood-louvered doors.

Hurrying, she doesn't bother closing the louver, and from her blissful perch she surveys the outer room. Yes, white marble walls and ceiling, black marble floor, but where's the soft-spoken woman in uniform waiting to dry Maggie's hands with a linen towel. And the sink? She's never seen the like. Its stone surround suffers stains from constant leakage.

Who cares? Relief can't be beat.

Now all I need—the L-word? Those yellow notes curl at the sight of herself in the mirror. *What would Mother say?*

No hope for her hair, Maggie washes her hands. She cups them, and sips the way she did from the farm hydrant. *Careful Maggs.* More trips to the Ritz would be inconvenient.

After a last slurp, she dries hands on her johnny, and with the phone cord retied, she climbs stairs to the lobby. The dowager and her cane have disappeared, but two plates remain on a small table by the empty chair, one with finger sandwiches laid out like a star, the other holds three petit fours set on a round doily, a fourth with a bite missing. Beside them, a full cup of tea cools.

Wasteful old bat! Maggie shakes her head in disgust. She sits in the vacated chair, knees together the way Mother taught her, and spreads the linen napkin. It slips off the fur. Unmindful, she lifts the cup, her little finger tucked under the handle. No extended pinkie for her. There's only so far she'll go to please Mother.

Mmmm, pond-scum sandwiches—watercress on white, the crusts sliced off. They alternate with deviled ham on wheat, so tender each bite slips right down, her strong teeth unchallenged. She savors the petit fours with their slick icing tongued off the roof of her mouth. Two dark...

Dark... ch..., I can never remember... oh, chocolate! Yes, the best. And two white, topped with pink sugared flowers.

All too soon, they're gone. She licks frosting from her fingers and sucks her teeth for the last speck. Not a smidgeon escapes, only the name.

From the floor she retrieves her napkin, dabs her mouth, and rising, saunters to the revolving door. Hank loves revolving doors almost as much as Maggie loves chocolate. She whirls around twice in his honor. *I miss him.*

She nods at the doorman's back as she glides past and re-crosses Arlington. On the other side, stroking her fur, she returns through the Garden fence.

A dim path winds into the park, and a few curves farther on, she watches a man caught in a pool of lamplight. He leans against the post. She stops. Her eyes narrow. On seeing her, he comes to attention, a tracker catching her scent.

Her muscles tighten. He zeros in, Maggie in his sights.

CHAPTER 9

HANK

Wednesday Evening

At the hospital, Hank crashes into Nana's room. "We're here Na..." The bed's empty. "Nana?"

And the chair. "Where are you?"

The triangle holes in his mask make it hard to see. She's got to cut them bigger, but she's not here.

He lifts the mask to his forehead. His front hairs stick up. "Ma!" He spins back to the hall. His cape hugs him. "Where's Nana?"

"No shenanigans, Hank." Ma pushes him through the doorway.

"Time to go, Mum," she says, as if she hadn't heard him. She looks in the bathroom. Checks behind the door. "Huh." Her forehead gets wrinkly.

Hank sinks to his knees by the bed. He rests his hand on the mattress. Leans down, looks under. "Too easy, she's a better hider than that."

Ma pulls at the zip-bag. The sheet comes with it. Hank helps. He shakes the bag. "Grizzly's gone."

More thinking wrinkles for Ma, then wham, she's at the nurse's desk, Hank beside her. He peeks over the desk. Jumps, jumps. "I bet she's back there."

"No." Ma has him by the neck.

"Discharged?" Ma says to the nurse. "She can't be."

The nurse zings her chair sideways. She picks up a clipboard. "Ten AM, see, right here." She taps the board.

"But I didn't..." Ma grips the desk with both hands. "She didn't have clothes!"

"She's got Grizzly."

"Security," the nurse says into the phone.

Ma fishes in her purse. Out comes her clam. She opens it. She dials. "Answer. Please answer."

Time for Major Amazing Man. Arms pumping, Hank's down the hall. "Not in here." He pushes open the next door. "Not here."

"Nana," he shouts. "Ollie Ollie Oxen Free. Where are you?"

Ma's right behind him. "Hank, this isn't a game."

"Stop!" The nurse is breathing fire. "Don't do that."

Three doors to go, and two guys in uniform show up. Jack Sprat and his buddy.

Sprat holds Ma's elbow. Buddy's got Hank by the cape.

"Leave it to us," he says, but he just stands there.

"You gotta find clues." Hank drags Buddy to Nana's room. "On the bed, see?"

"Good work kid." The man holds up Grizzly's bag. "We'll do this. You and your ma wait in the lobby."

In the elevator, the guys keep tight to their elbows. In the hall, too. All the way to the waiting room.

The plastic chair makes snappy noises when Hank jiggles his legs. His mask itches less around his neck.

Ma dials her cell. "Shi...." Hank knows the whole word, though she doesn't say it. It means she's big-time pissed. The clam slams. She stamps her foot. "Dead."

"NANA's dead?"

"Not Nana, she's fine," Ma says. "The *phone's* dead."

A man with stripes on his uniform sleeve taps a clipboard. "You're looking for Margaret Colton?"

Ma jumps to her feet. "You found her?"

"This your signature?" He points at a piece of paper.

"Yes, but she... but I..."

"Please stay calm, we're searching. The best thing for you is to go home. We'll call you."

"Want me to kick him?" Hank whispers.

"I'm calling the police," she says, but she can't; the clam's dead.

"Don't worry, she's here somewhere," the guy says. "So many halls, old folks get confused. You go on home."

"No, we have to keep looking."

"You can't be barging into people's rooms."

"We won't, just halls, I promise." And Ma's off into the crowds. Hank trips at her heels.

Ma lied. She pokes her head in this door. In that door. A woman sleeps with her mouth open. A man on a bedpan, "Hey, what the…" Ma ducks out. On to the next.

Too many doors.

Hank drags.

Night doesn't slow her at first, but their two doughnuts wear off along with Ma's second coffee. Her face is wet. Hank rubs his eyes, right when Sprat, Buddy, and the guy with stripes block the way.

"Enough now," Stripes says. "You're being disruptive, and your boy belongs at home."

Ma looks at Hank. She checks her watch. "But I can't…"

"The hospital's on alert. We'll find your mother. Now, think of your child. Go home."

The men edge Ma and Hank into the lobby. Ma makes a last stand. "Call the police, please."

"I'm sure that won't be necessary. We're doing a room-to-room search. She's probably asleep in an extra bed. We'll keep her for the night." He crowds Ma toward the door.

"If you don't find her by the time I get home, I'm calling the police."

He pats Hank's head. Hank ducks and puts a shoulder to the revolving door. "Three times around is best." Ma yanks him out after one.

In the parking garage, up one level, down the next, "*Where's* the car?"

"Bad guys got it?"

"No Hank, no bad guys. The car's here somewhere, and so is Nana."

"In the garage?" Hank gets on all fours. He eyeballs underneath the cars. "Nope."

"Not Nana." Ma takes a deep breath. "She's in the hospital, or maybe she went shopping."

That's silly, Nana hates shopping.

Ma checks both sides of the next level. She makes a TSSSH, sound. Ben says it's her pressure-cooker noise. She's not fooling Hank. He's heard the real word, lots.

"Nana might shop for ice cream," he says, "or cookies."

Finally, at the highest level, Ma unlocks the van. In the van, parking ticket ready, she reads, "Pay first." She beats the steering wheel with her fists.

Amazing Man stays amazingly quiet in his booster seat.

At home, Ma doesn't yell. Not at Hank, when he tosses his jacket on the front room sofa. She always wants him to hang it by the back door. She doesn't yell at the others either. They're in their rooms. Cage Rest, Nana calls it.

Sasha's trumpet screeches. Ben keeps his bedroom door shut. He wears earphones, always. Funny way to be in charge.

Hank hates when Ben is king of the castle.

❧❦

The first time Ben sat for Hank and Sasha, he pulled out a pistol. He said, "You do what I say, or I'll shoot."

"Nit-wit." Sasha turned her back. "Dad wouldn't give you a real gun."

"Yeah, well, he promised for my sixteenth birthday, he'll give me his."

The pistol scared Hank. It really looked real. Real enough to get Ben sent home from school the very next day.

Ma hid it. Hank felt much safer, even if it was pretend. But then Ben said, "You're gonna wake up dead someday." After that Hank wore his mask and cape to bed. He couldn't be too careful.

❧❦

In the kitchen, busy at the phone, Ma stretches the curly cord straight. It pulls her back to the box on the wall by the window. She holds the receiver out. She shouts at it, "Roger, where *are* you?" That's Uncle Rog she's after. She slams the handle on the hook.

To Hank, for the fifth time, she says, "Nana's at the hospital, so don't worry. And don't worry the others." That means he better worry.

She stabs the numbers. She waits.

Hank needs to search; they both... "Come on Ma, let's find her."

"I'm calling the police."

"If Nana's fine, why police?"

"Please, Hank, go play…." She points toward the front room. "And no TV."

Hank settles his cape on his shoulders. He fiddles his mask. He zags down the hall, past plastic sheets covering the living room door. The dining room, too. They're taped too tight to peek.

Ma's been fixing stuff her way, since Dad's "on vacation." No one's allowed in but carpenters, plumbers, and a painter. Doing what? It's hard to find out anything when everything's changing.

Is it wrong to listen when Uncle Rog and Ma talk? It's the only way to know what's what. Like Dad's "vacation."

And Ma calling the police: "…yes, missing…blue eyes, sharp nose, probably wearing…"

In the front room, Hank flops on the sofa in front of the big windows. His butt sinks through the center cushion where Zip has dug a pit. Zip does that when he's left alone.

Heading for China, Ma says. He hates being by himself. She says dogs don't need alone-time like some people. Uncle Rog says Ma needs more than most.

Hank prefers Zip's pit to the armchair. It's like an inner tube. His legs hang over the edge, arms flat on the side cushions. He floats. The lightning flash on his shirt glows.

His fingers talk in the lake. He whispers to the fish, "Snapper! Snapper! Watch-it. Spikes all over the turtle's shell, mouth wide—Gonna-getcha."

The high voice of a sunfish, "No! No!" Splashing.

Hank's butt is deep in the pit. His legs whirl the air. He beats the cushions with his arms.

The sunnies squeak, "Look, in the sky!" Hank scans the ceiling. "Yeah, Major Amazing Man." The sunnies cheer. Major Amazing flies with the birds, talks to the fish.

Hank's right-hand swoops. "He dives!"

"AAaaaa!" The snapper flips on his back. He chokes. He glugs to the bottom.

Ma's voice rises from the kitchen, talking to herself again, "She'll be the death of me."

Wow, if Ma goes dead, Hank could live with Nana. He knows how that would be: lots of hide and seek, sitting on Nana's couch, reading by firelight. They'd read *A Night in the Museum* till her big clock bongs more times than Hank has fingers. And Chunky Monkey ice cream for breakfast!

But if Ma's dead... Exactly where is *dead*?

It's wherever Hockey-Boy's guinea pig lives. Ben hates Hank calling him Hockey-Boy. He does it all the time. So does Nana. But Ben never knuckles Nana's head.

∞ ❧

Hank's stomach complains. With all the sunnies safe, he zigs back into the kitchen. "Ma, can I have..."

Ma looks out the dark window. She bangs her head with her fists. "No. I have to...I have..."

"Have to get dinner?"

Ma dials the phone as if he isn't there.

"OK, I'll get it myself."

He hopscotches over black and white tiles to the tall cabinet, opens it. On a stool, he reaches to the "no-no-not-now" shelf and snitches a giant bag of peanut M&Ms. All the food groups, Nana always says: protein, something green, something yellow, something red. Blue? Not on the list. He eats it anyway and fills his pants pockets.

He hops off the stool, and his cape flies up behind him. Ma presses a hand to her forehead. "...no, Rog, not that gone. Disappeared, she..." Ma all frantic-face. "They claimed I..."

Hank stands on one foot, pulls his tongue. Inside out this time?

"...YES, I called her doctor AND the police."

"Ma." Hank tugs on her sleeve. "Are they looking?"

"Twenty-four hours!" She chokes. "...incompetent, I told them...Not legally, but...They said confusion isn't a crime."

Hank slips under the taut phone cord. "What's incompliment?"

"I can't just stay home." She twists the cord. "Someone has to find her."

Hank tugs harder at the hem of her jacket. "That's what I'm saying."

"Oh Hank, I'm trying..." She puts her hand over the mouthpiece. "Nana needs help, and you can help by doing your homework."

"I don't have homework." He hooks the curled cord with his little finger. "I'm five." He jerks it. "Remember?"

"Then get to bed."

Hank bounces wall-to-wall to the stairs. He stops at the newel post.

Pieces of talk float down the hall: "...her blood pressure... angina... pills."

Nana calls those pills, "My Dynamite." They're in every room of her house. The littlest pain and Nana's s'posed to take one. Hank wanted one when he stubbed his toe on a rock at the lake. It really-really hurt.

"Not that kind of pain." Ma told him. How many kinds of pain are there?

"...that's not all." Ma, still in the kitchen. "It'll kill her if Clyde...no, he's not back."

Hank sticks his head in the front room. The armchair where Clyde's been sleeping has only a circle of black hairs. Maybe Hank can slip out, too. But he'll need help.

He runs two flights up to Ben's room, bangs through the door. Zip jumps on him—long lost boy, licks his whole face.

Hank talks through Zip's beard, "Ben, you've got to help me."

"Beat it, Pea-brain." Ben kicks the door, shutting Hank and Zip in the hall.

"Thanks, Hockey-Boy," he hollers. "I'll do it myself."

Strong as Major Amazing is, he needs a weapon against Nana-nappers. He needs...yes, Ben's pretend gun. It might fool them.

Ma says it could fool the police and get Ben shot. That's why she hid it.

Hid it where?

Dad had a pistol, one of those secrets Hank wasn't supposed to know. Ma had yelled, "Get rid of the damn thing."

Ben's toy was different. Hidden, it would keep till he got big. When he knew how to be safe.

Real or not, it was better than nothing.

Hank nips down to Ma's bedroom. At her dresser, he runs his hands under clothes in the drawer. Nope.

Dad kept his gun on top of the closet. Another not-so-secret secret. Ben's too?

Hank drags a chair across the carpet to the closet. Not high enough. He gets an ancient yellow-pages from the bookshelf. Almost there. White-pages on top, and holding the chair-back, he climbs. Good thing Ma never throws anything away.

Reaching into the shelf, he pats his hand past Ma's sweaters. He stretches to the back, and *Bingo*, his fingers close on something cold just as the phonebooks slip.

Down go the yellows and whites, Hank, the chair, and the cold thing. He hits the carpet with a thud. Hank hopes Ma's too busy to notice.

He examines, yes, a pistol. *Yikes!* This isn't Ben's. It's a snub-nosed six-shooter like on TV. *Dad's.* His finger on the trigger, Hank waggles the thing. It's heavy.

Shiny edges of bullets catch the light. "Cripe," he whispers. TV teaches all sorts of things. Like how to know when a gun's loaded.

In his room, he slides the pistol behind his belt buckle, the metal even colder on his belly, and refits the mask over his eyes. He tightens the cape. Under his yellow sweatshirt, his chest swells. He rubs the lightning bolt. He pumps his muscles. Stronger every second, Amazing Man has it all, including Sasha's sparkly red shoes.

He didn't steal them. She gave them. They pinched her toes.

Better than Ma's GPS. In Boston or in Oz, two clicks will get him home. Too big, they clop down the hall.

The gun digs with every step. "OW." He limps. If he had a holster, he'd tuck it under his arm.

His jacket pocket will do, but first he needs something with Nana's smell. Zip's no bloodhound, just a pointer known for pointing out cake. And cats. "Come on boy."

From under the futon in Ma's office, Hank finds an old sock. Long and thin, it's not Uncle Rog's, so it has to be Nana's. He waves it against Zip's nose. "Find her boy, find her," he says, and they run for the door. He throws on his jacket, the cape on top, and tucks the pistol in his pocket.

Ma's voice comes from the kitchen. "—yes, go look."

"Great!" he says and runs down the hall. More from Ma, "Start at the hospital. Hurry, Rog."

Holding the latch, Hank closes the door super-quiet. Zip hauls him into the dark yard and down the path, sniff-sniff over the sidewalk, into the street. Hank's cape flaps. The neighbors' lights hardly touch him. His bright blue cape doesn't show.

The yellow sweatshirt hides under his jacket along with the green lightning bolt. Nana had sewed it. "Glue won't hold," she'd said. "Do it right or not at all."

Zip finds Nana's smell, and they're off. "I'm coming Nana!"

No sooner off, Zip suddenly halts, spinning Hank by the leash in the wrong direction. "No, Zip." Zip noses all around the hydrant. He lifts his leg. Hank jerks the leash. "Stop it, we're looking for Nana."

"Oh, cripe." He tips his face at the sky. Rain spits.

He shoves the mask on top of his head. Elastic tangles the hair behind his ear. "Ouch." Major Amazing shouldn't say *ouch*. He pulls the elastic. It hurts more.

Headlights come up the street. Tires hiss. And passing, the taillights flash. At the corner they disappear. He should follow them to Boston, but Hockey-Boy says hitching beats walking. Hank balls a fist, thumb out.

Zip freezes. He points, nose out straight, but, *Oh no*, it's not Nana. On the neighbor's sidewalk... a small ghost? Hank tries not to believe in ghosts. He pats his gun, for all the good it would do.

Oh phew, it's just the devil's sidekick, Fluffy, a cat with ratty white fur who doesn't mind rain.

Fluffy drives Zip nuts. Mostly, Zip whines from the safety of the front room, but tonight, he barks his brains out. Fluffy turns her back.

The first time they met, Fluffy played super-fly. She landed on Zip. She dug in her claws and rode him home. No one messes with Fluffy.

From behind Hank, a hand snatches his hair. It hurts worse than the elastic. "Gotcha, you little brat."

That voice. It's Mrs. Garibaldi—Fluffy's "Mummy." She yanks.

"OW." Hank drops the leash.

Zip rushes Fluffy. Hissing, she swipes his nose, and Zip takes off for the house, tail between his legs.

Mrs. G shifts her pinch to Hank's ear. The other hand at his back like a gun, she marches him into her house.

Inside, she keeps hold of his ear, picks up her weird phone, antique, Ma says, same as Mrs. G. She dials the numbers in a circle.

All witchy, she hollers into the handle, "Do you know where your son is?"

CHAPTER 10

MAGGIE

Wednesday Night

Up from leaning against the lamppost, the man waves. He strides toward Maggie, arms out. Beneath the furry coat her legs root to the asphalt. Her chest ignites. His arms spread wider, ready to catch her. There's something in the light of his face, his excitement. An open-mouthed grin. His startling happiness.

Bobby? Maggie's feet uproot. Fingers at her mouth, she prays it's her brother. He'll take her home, no need for a yellow brick road, or even wingtips. He'll know the way to the T. She remembers the Red Line. The Porter stop? Only a short walk after that.

She can see it already, her porch with its leaded-glass star, the light suspended from the ceiling, warm and welcoming no-matter the weather.

But... She'd be the intruder, the creepy person the star keeps off the porch. She'll be a stranger, closed out of her own house, rejected by the one thing she counts on. Home should always be home, and they've sold it.

Well, almost. Bobby could help with... with...

Lawyer, right, the lawyer. And now his building, hard to find in the dark. She can't see his giant window. Near the garden, the windows are too small. So look on the other side. The Common side. *Try... Where's Bobby got to?*

She has to find him, the lawyer. Her porch star should never kiss a stranger's cheek. She can't allow another's key to tumble in her lock. She won't let the heavy door, swinging wide, embrace another's entry. Never will the newel post wrap itself in the scent of some other woman's coat.

But my treasures! Clair might sell my portraits. The ones that scared babysitters when Maggie, Dan, and the kids lived in the South End, those gold-framed primitives that no one but Maggie loves.

છ૭૪

In her own house, her family had hung on the walls, keeping Maggie company at dinner, them stiff in nineteenth, or was it eighteenth, century attire. They whispered secrets. Great-Great-Grandfather Helmsworth was the loudest, his barely restrained leer at odds with the upright collar, cinched with a black cravat.

His tightly-laced wife berated him, her dark brows lowered, while their nubile ward in off-the-shoulder velvet looked at the ceiling, innocent to the end.

Without shame, Maggie eavesdropped on their wrangling. They never questioned her evening martini or asked why she hadn't finished her taxes. No raised eyebrows at ice cream; they had more important considerations.

Clair, too, has more important considerations: the absent Rick for instance. *Rick the dick, a fulltime worry.* Maggie's fault; she should have stopped the marriage, but she wanted to believe that love conquered all. *Pure pie in the sky.* He went from football to horses to cockfights. Rick was a shark without teeth, except when putting the bite on Clair.

She'll get rid of all my favorites. The rugs, the glass-front shelves, books and books and books. "Mum won't need these in The Home," would be her excuse.

Maggie had seen the brochures for the old people's home mixed in with the bills on Clair's dining room table, the photos spiffed-up to look appealing instead of the reality of cramped rooms, plastic bureaus, hospital beds, the linoleum halls where wheelchairs dribble by. And the horrible olive walls. *The only acceptable place for olive is in a martini.*

I could use one now.

છ૭૪

Suspicious, Clair had checked out those places after Maggie's solo adventure in the Caribbean. Clair was the one to send her off. "A rest will do you good. You haven't been yourself."

She felt like herself. A reader. A portrait painter. A fashion writer, before... *Arthritics, I think.* The Caribbean heat would help her swollen joints. She'd get back to drawing, a pencil and pad in her fanny pack.

Clair and Rog bought the tickets, a present for her seventy-somethingth birthday. Maggie didn't need persuading. No one passes up a free vacation. And her friend Agnes wanted to join her; in fact, Clair insisted. She even paid Agnes's way. "You'll have more fun with a friend."

Too bad Agnes got sick. Though things had turned interesting, with Maggie being on her own

At first, she refused to go boating. She sat alone on the beach, and that's where she met the man in black. Who wears black in the Islands?

On her third day, Maggie woke from a beach nap and on the next towel, there he was. *In a hooded robe, no less.* She'd seen him in the hotel dining room, plate in hand, an unattached male. *Black-suited, then. No loud-patterned shirt for him.*

Hardly Maggie's type. And if he were, she'd never consider another marriage. No man could top Dan. Friend and husband. She misses his smile, misses the way, when sitting in company, he'd secretly graze her thigh with his little finger; the way his aura stayed with her across a room, across the country. Even across the ocean, she felt him beside her the way she feels him now, across the stygian river.

She could drive herself crazy thinking about those nights before children. It took nothing to set Maggie and Dan rushing upstairs to the bedroom, ripping off clothes as they went. No time to draw the blinds.

Hurried hands at buttons, a zipper, the bra hooks, hopping out of socks, body parts desperate to be touched, they'd fallen skin to hot skin on the cool sheets. *Ahhh.*

So why did she even bother to look? For Clair, of course. Clair had so much of her life left for love.

Maggie couldn't see her with this one. He needed more meat on his bones, though something about him seemed familiar. From TV, perhaps. No, no one paid him any attention, so probably not.

Maggie, on her towel, ignored him. It wasn't easy with him a mere three feet away, sitting cross-legged under his robe.

"Hi, Maggie," he said.

"You know my name?"

The hint of a smile crinkled around his eyes. "I'm good with names." He pushed off his hood, waved at swimmers, and nodded at a lifeguard ankle deep in the bluest-blue sea. His glance covered shell collectors as they scuffed the white sand, their shoulders crisping in the sun. "I know them all," he said and flashed a pearly grin.

Rolling onto her side, she faced him, finding his dark-eyed attention disconcerting at first. He yawned and stretched long limbs. His robe opened, exposing his torso, even skinnier than she thought. Considering his shark-belly skin, the island sun would do him a world of good. And a little more hair wouldn't hurt. His was buzzed to a shadow, a phrenologist's dream.

Clair would like his chest where a smattering of hair gathered, running a path over a tight belly and into his Speedo. The suit's narrow cloth stretched, cupping fulsome jewels. She wondered if he augmented. Jeremy always said men are vainer than women.

The man's eyes wandered over her body. *Fair's fair, sort of.* She couldn't complain, though it seemed odd. No one since Chuckey Wilson, the new boy in eighth grade, had looked with such hunger. Back then, her T-shirt had been soaked in the rain, visible nipples saluting Chuckey's bug-eyed luck.

Now wait a minute. Maggie frowned. *Who looks like that at a woman my age?* Flirting was one thing, but...

He leaned on an elbow. That smile again, possessively friendly. "Not to worry," he said. His eyes searched hers, deep and plundering.

"You're making fun of me."

"Never." He laughed and fished in his robe pockets. "Could I borrow…?"

No neighborly cup of sugar here, what could he want? Her bikini top?

Her turn to laugh; she wouldn't dream of wearing a bikini, ever.

"It's not your bathing costume," he said as if he'd read her mind.

"Costume indeed." She snorted. "I'm not that out of date. And what about you in your black robe?"

"Sun allergy," he said and wrapped his robe close as if he'd caught a chill.

"So why the beach?"

His eyes wandered over the calm water, checking swimmers bobbing the surface. He tapped two fingers on his knee and suddenly, out on the water, a distant swimmer thrashed the surface. The man leapt to his feet. Stripping off his robe, he plunged, long strokes taking him toward the flailing arms. Late off the mark, lifeguards followed into action.

Beach-goers crowded the water's edge, watching in horror as the arms sank and the water calmed well before rescuers closed in.

Afterward a lifeguard told her, "Dr. D., *my friend in black,* reached the guy, but too late." No more details. The staff wasn't supposed to talk.

It took three days of plastered-on smiles and free champagne to bubble the island spirit back to life. Funny how, on the islands, forgetting was encouraged. She needed to take that island ease to the states and share it with Clair.

The third day on the beach, Doc said, "The wind's perfect for parasailing. Let's go." He spread his arms toward the water dotted with boats. Three of them launched skiers into the sky where they dangled from rainbow-colored kites.

"You're making fun again." Sitting on her towel, she hugged her knees. "I've had enough death. I'm not flying, not even the friendliest sky, without a plane."

"Weren't you the motorcyclist?" He reached for her hand.

"I was young and foolish."

"You're still the same person, come on."

She dug her toes in the sand. "I don't think so."

"People your age do it all the time," he persisted. "Live a little."

Others did and so finally, on the last day of vacation, she relented. She took his twiggy fingers in hers, and before she knew it, she was kiting high above the beach.

Below her, the dot of their speedboat zipped parallel to the white beach, the whole green island small in a shimmering sea.

She may as well have been twenty, hair flying, legs dancing in the rush of warm wind, her new friend snapping pictures.

All too soon the boat circled back. Slowing, it dropped her gently right on the beach where she'd started. She should have said *yes* before.

She wasn't too old. Old is a state of mind, and she wouldn't put up with it. Not anymore.

Doc waved the camera as she landed. "Lots of good shots."

She snatched the camera's strap before he could object, "Let me take you," and swung it up, snapping away.

"No, no," he said pressing a finger to the lens. "The camera doesn't like me."

The next afternoon as she stepped into a taxi for the airport, he rushed from the hotel. "I didn't have time to develop these," he said and handed her a roll of film. *Now, who's the old fashioned one?* With cool lips, he kissed her cheek. "Look for me. I'm coming your way, Lex maybe."

"Good, my daughter's in Lexington. You'll like Clair."

On landing in Boston, she followed the crowd to baggage claim.

"Mum, Mum!" Clair waved. "Over here."

Maggie worked a path to Clair beside the carousel. "Where's Agnes?" Clair asked.

"Couldn't come. Sick at the last minute." Maggie watched for her bag in the jumble of luggage. "Too bad, Doc could have fixed her up."

Maggie shouldn't have mentioned Doc. Clair dug at her until she spilled.

"Foolishness," Clair said. Driving the car, she gave Maggie a sharp glance.

"You don't believe me!"

"Mum, really? Dressed in black? Parasailing?" She kept her eyes on the highway.

Brat. "I have pictures."

"Stay for a visit," Clair said. "A quick one. I want to see pictures." So chirpy and friendly, and Maggie fell for it.

That very afternoon Maggie took the film to a camera shop. The doorbell dinged as she entered. "One hour, right?" She passed the canister to the girl behind the counter.

"Yes, you can wait." She indicated a chair.

No way could she sit still. Anticipation worked her fingers. She bit her nails.

Time limped by, and finally back at the counter, the cashier rang her up.

Hurrying across the street, she couldn't wait, and opened the envelope. She pulled out the pictures.

Oh, black and white, what a disappointment. She missed the yellow, red, and blue of the billowing kite, and her friend. She wanted Clair to see him. There again, disappointment. The pictures were out of focus.

At least the important thing showed, Maggie lifting out of the water, picture after picture till she became a dot in the sky.

Seeing herself felt like a resurrection. *No dust on these old bones.*

She had it, undisputable proof. What a triumph, to see the skeptical look drain from Clair's eyes; and with that thought her toe hit the curb. Her ankle twisted, flinging her and the pictures into a puddle. White lightning ripped through her head.

After the blur of the hospital, Maggie landed at Clair's. Week after week, Maggie reminded herself how lucky she was to be there, but it felt like eons.

Most likely, eons for Clair, too. Maggie slept in Clair's bed, while Clair slept on the floor where Maggie would step if she dared set foot out of bed. *Worse than Zip.*

Sometimes Maggie forgot how she got there to begin with. The *why* of the crutches seemed hard to remember as well.

"Why?" Maggie said at dinner. Trumpet-Girl snickered around a mouthful of mashed potato. The others kept to their dining room manners even though they all ate in the kitchen.

Clair sighed. "You broke your leg."

"And!" said Ben.

"And hit your head," Trumpet-Girl answered.

"You thought you were a cockroach." Hockey-Boy convulsed. Clair kicked him under the table, as if Maggie couldn't tell. They hid smiles in their napkins, except Hank.

"You flew in the sky," he said, "a paratrooper, and you tripped on the sidewalk; it's not fair." At least Hank believed.

"Too bad about the pictures." Clair shook her head, a plate in each hand as she cleared. "Just gray shapes."

"My pictures, where..." Maggie planted her hands on the table and stood.

"Nooo," Hank shouted.

Pain shot through her leg. She sat hard. "I forgot."

"You remember the man in black," Trumpet-Girl said. "Who was that?"

Clair frowned at the child.

"Woo, woo!" Ben chanted. "Nana's got a boyfriend."

Clair's frown turned scowl. "We're not talking about that."

The ostrich effect. *It's a miracle Clair can breathe with her head up her...in the sand so deep.*

When Maggie switched to a walking brace, she had a mission: lighten Clair's load. First, the bed. But Clair wouldn't take it even when Maggie beat the floor with her cane.

Laundry, she could do that. With Clair off at the grocer's, Maggie got to it, dirty clothes already thrown at the bottom of the stairwell.

Pile on pile, a plethora of aromatic gym shorts, school shirts and pants dribbled with chocolate, panties with grass stains, jeans without. One poorly aimed bra hung from the light on the stairwell's second floor. Zip lay on the pile, better than any mattress he commandeered.

From the edge of the pile, Maggie dragged an armload to the laundry room, just off the kitchen. She sorted lights from darks, loaded evenly around the agitator, searched the shelf for liquid soap, and found a family-size container among Clair's many boxes and bottles.

No cap to measure, careless. But capable-Clair had an eye for amounts.

When Maggie did small loads at home, a dollop sufficed, so this would take several dollops. She clicked around the dial to twelve and squeezed a green stream into the machine as it filled. The lid closed, the agitator grumbled to life, and the dog stayed for a nap on the remaining pile. This gave Maggie plenty of time to nap herself. She retreated to Clair's room.

"Bloody hell!" Clair's full-volume yell ended the nap.

Maggie ventured down to the first-floor hall. The dog fled through her legs. She scrabbled at the wall, barely staying upright.

Clair with bags and bags of groceries, including a chocolate cake and twenty-five pounds of flour dangling from her arms, stood before the kitchen door. An avalanche of soapsuds billowed forth.

The suds engulfed her feet. Clair stood transfixed. "Bloody hell."

She lifted her face toward the ceiling. "Haaaank." A natural assumption; he loved playing with suds in the sink.

"It wasn't Hank," Maggie said, coming into the flood behind Clair.

They waded into the kitchen, bubbles to their ankles. Clair heaved the bags onto the island counter, then slogged to the open laundry room door. The bottle, with a green tear sliding down its side, stood on the dryer. If it had fingers, it would have pointed at Maggie.

"Dish soap!" Clair clenched her coif in both fists, the white streaks increasing every day. "You put dish soap in the washer."

Brother Bobby would have laughed.

✠

In the park Maggie finds herself staring at the man running toward her. *Damn, not Bobby.* As he advances, fast footsteps sound behind her. Her hackles rise. The steps close in and, too late to run, visions of freedom fade. A woman's voice overtakes her, "Thank heaven, I thought I'd lost you." Maggie waits for Clair's hand, the grab on her shoulder.

Grazing her arm, the woman blows past and into the man's swinging embrace. Maggie chokes on an in-breath, a moment of weakness loosening her legs. She bends, feet spread, hands to her knees, and shakes her head. *Better you than me, Sweetie.* Yet she envies the couple's certainty and the vision of their days to come.

Her own days to come look murkier than Oz, and she envies Dorothy, with the farm waiting at the end of her wanderings, Auntie Em's arms open, Dorothy no worse for wear than a bump on the noggin.

But Maggs, remember… she has two sets of open arms waiting. She admits, their intentions aren't bad. They aren't.

They want to take care. *Sure, like gangsters take care of a witness.* A pair of cement overshoes, Maggie sinking into the comforts of Boston Harbor. Actually, that might be preferable. *Where's Whitey Bulger when I need him?*

But here she is like the inconvenient witness, sneaking through evening dark, trying to reach the Common side of the park. Take the bridge first, but between Maggie and the bridge, right there, glowing blue in the distance, is a cluster of black holes. Those unlit places, a girl's undoing, or so the old biddies at boarding school told her. The housemother terrified Maggie and her cronies with tales of sex-starved specters lying in wait; those with a nose for girls foolish enough to wander from their elders' ever-loving protection. Nevertheless, with easily-spotted cops on the bridge, she steps into the closest shadow and keeps still.

No one in the shadows has a taste for crones. *Being old has its perks.*

These cops are not the protectors she'd always counted on. These hunt her. The blue light of the bridge on their caps casts a dead space where eyes and nose should be. Only the flash of their teeth shows as her hunters laugh, their attention cast east, then north to west, south, before walking over the pedestrian bridge.

At the other end, they saunter on, one swinging his billy club. She waits until the pair crosses Charles Street. They enter the Common, disappearing toward Beacon and the capital.

She mounts the bridge. Exposed in the blue light, she feels a tiny moth dinking around in her chest so unsettling as it touches the underside of her breastbone. It's a whispered warning she can't quite place.

The cold is another matter. She remembers the trick, and turns her coat again, fur to skin, warm as a bear.

Onward Maggs. Above her the last of the clouds scud by, and the moon nods, his mouth in open surprise.

"Yes, it's me, Maggs." She waves.

A sign? Signs are always there; she only has to open her eyes and know them for what they are. She would trust a pheasant. In this case, the moon will have to do as it nods at the path to the Common.

Coattails flowing, Maggie sets out from the bridge and pushes on toward the fence with its iron gate. The New World Symphony fills her head until a stream of metallic reds, blues, and silvers halts her. Four lanes with white stripes between— the torrent of Charles Street traffic.

Her eyes on the field at the other side, she slides a foot carefully off the curb, the way she'd step into a whitewater stream. Luckily, she finds the asphalt smooth, no holes to twist her ankle, no rocks biting her precious wingtips.

Cars blow past, leaving little space between, but she knows the way. *It's like jump-rope.* She rocks back and forth the way she did on the playground, her friends swinging a long clothesline, inviting her to jump into the spin.

Before she got the knack, their fast rope slapped her head. It's all in the timing. *The double rope, now that's a challenge.*

As the cars flash by she shifts her weight, back foot to front, *Wait.* She watches for the break, front foot to back, *Wait for it. WAIT...* "NOW!" And she jumps.

CHAPTER 11

CLAIR

Wednesday Night

Sweat beads her forehead. Kitchen lights burn. Clair shivers in her own private tundra. Her eyes sting.

No, she won't cry, not with Hank in and out of the kitchen. She's got to be a walking, breathing Stonehenge. No slip of her stiff upper lip. Her behavior in the hospital was bad enough.

Closing her eyes, all she can see is Mum on the streets, how the dark closes in, how the cold seeps deeper with every crawling minute. And rain.

Slippage isn't the word for Mum, not anymore. She's in free-fall, and the police...they don't seem to care.

The law's long arms should hold her, buoy her. The men (in this case, they are men) should be on her side, their enfolding hands scooping her mother up from the mire.

Until this moment, Clair had always loved the city, even with its grit. But what weighs on her now is the city's looming presence, the high buildings looking down with depraved indifference. Arms rigid, the phone on the wall, every muscle in her body seems frozen. It's hard to unclench the receiver.

Roger is the man who cares. He does. But he can't or won't believe Mum's incapacity. At least he's searching, despite his denial.

And the police, they've got to do more. Without pills, Mum could...

The phone in her hand squawks its off-the-hook irritation. She slams down the receiver and sprints for the stairs. She needs sneakers. She can't search in heels, sensible or not.

Could it be only this morning she thought order had been restored, her worries at an end?

෨෬

While Clair drove to the hospital that morning, set to pick up her mother, she'd reveled in the end of panic—those runs from Lexington to Cambridge, losing track of the kids. Hank especially.

Mum would finally be safe, no more dread every time the phone rang. No more Hank abandoned at school, imagining she'd been kidnapped.

The last time Clair came late, Hank's teacher tapped her watch until she saw Mum sitting in the passenger seat, drenched through her nightgown. Ms. Hegger must have suspected elder abuse. In her shoes, Clair would have. And in some ways, that's what it was, Clair as bad as Rog, postponing the misery she dreaded inflicting, putting off facing her mother as she gave the final verdict. Sold. Postponing their confrontation came down to misplaced love. Or perhaps, pure cowardice.

Just talking to Rog wasn't easy. "This is too dangerous," she'd told him.

"Constant care, we have to." Someone had to be the bad guy, and it always came down to Clair.

Mostly, Rog hid in Curry House, convinced the doctor's words would eventually be right: "Her brain will develop new pathways. She's fine." Seeing reality wasn't his strong suit. It wasn't the doctor's, either.

If Rog had been with her that blowy afternoon, it might have made a difference. Minutes before Clair had to pick up Hank, the kitchen phone rang. Essie, their mother's neighbor in Cambridge. Again.

"You know, she's in the yard."

Oh, God, Clair could hear thunder through the line.

"She's still in her nightdress. Looking for the cat, but he's in the window watching her." Of course he was. "And it's starting to pour."

"I'm on my way; please, get her inside."

"She won't; you have to come."

Hank in the lurch again. Clair ran, her purse forgotten. Driving one handed, she pulled her phone from her pocket and dialed Roger's number; ordinarily not something she'd do. His voicemail picked up. Damn it. She didn't bother messaging. He never checked.

Hank would be sitting on the sidewalk conjuring the worst. She sped down the highway, windshield wipers on high, and called the school.

Pulling up in front of her mother's house, she could see Mum still in the yard. It was a good thing the day had been warm for October.

Her mother prowled around the garden, deadheading chrysanthemums. Essie stood in her open door across the street. "I told her the cat's in the house." She waved both hands, dismissing the whole event, and closed the door.

"Come out of the rain, Mum." Clair hurried across the yard. "Clyde's inside."

"I know," Mum said. "He locked the door." Her way of saying she went out without her keys. An old habit, even when Clair was little.

Her mother's hair ran long and wet from its untwisted bun, a gray flow over the shoulders of her flowered nightgown, her feet in Bean boots.

"Change your clothes. Hurry now." They headed for the house. Keys—she didn't have her purse. She patted her pockets. Only the car key.

Like mother, like daughter? Now that was scary.

Clair opened the passenger door. "Get in, Mum. Hank's waiting."

Clair cranked up the heat.

৵৩

On her way to pick up her mother at the hospital, it never occurred to Clair that things could get worse. She watched a disorganized 'V' of ducks fly west. West? Their sense of direction

81

was out of whack, and she smiled. Smug little twit, thinking she had *her* ducks in the right formation.

ℰℭℬℭℜ

Now, "worse" doesn't begin to describe it. Ready to search, sneakers laced, at the back door with coat, car key, purse— Oh, Hank.

She has to tuck him in, reassure him, Nana's fine. She's Fiiiiiiiine.

Fiiiiiiiine works no better at calming than Ooooooom. It does for others, so she'd have to try meditation again when... Her stomach jitters.

"Ben," she calls up the stairs. He'll sit for the others. "Hank?" He must be in his room.

The phone rings. She's found, thank God. Clair rips the receiver off the hook. "Is she..."

A woman's angry voice, "Do you know where your son is?"

"Son? What?" Clair leans into the phone. She hopes closer attention will clear the muddle. "Hello, hello! Who is this?"

"Your boy, the one in the mask, and that dog, they attacked my Fluffy." The line clicks.

Clair peers out the kitchen window, and sure enough, there's Hank with Mrs. Garibaldi coming down her porch steps. She has him by the ear, his neck bent.

Clair opens the front door. Zip rushes in, jumps on the front room sofa, breath steaming the window, and barks at Fluffy on the sidewalk. The cat rubs herself on Mrs. G.'s ankles.

"If you can't keep track of them," Mrs. G shouts across the street, "you shouldn't have children." She marches Hank to the curb and lets him go.

He straightens, walking backward. "You have to understand," he tells her, loud enough for the deafest ear. "Ma's got a lot on her mind." He smooths his cow-licked hair. "My Nana's been napped, like a kid, only she's a grownup." Hank opens his jacket wide. He likes to display his lightning bolt. "Me and Zip were on her trail when ..."

"Young man, tall tales will get you nowhere. I should call the police."

He stops on the walk to the house. "Ma says they're useless, that's why I..."

"So, you've been in trouble before." She shakes a finger at him. "Leave Fluffy be or I'll call the Children's Home." She eyes his sparkly shoes. "They'll want to know why a boy wears girl's clothes."

CHAPTER 12

MAGGIE

Wednesday Night

Horns blare as Maggie leaps across the stream of oncoming traffic. She lands on a white dotted line. *Maggs, you did it, you're safe.*

Behind her a car blows past, forcing her coat tight to her backside. With a whoosh, another car flashes by in front, and in passing leaves a moment of space behind. She hops to the next white line.

Bee-bee-bee-beeping horns build to a crescendo. Her heart drums in a dissonant chorus. The grass of the Common beckons.

She gathers coattails for the next jump, but a black car bears down too fast. She waits. As it flashes by, the driver tips his black hat, his face pale as the underside of a slug, almost bluish. He grins, an eager participant in her game of traffic leapfrog. His mirror skims the front of her coat.

Her arms shoot up, hands above her head. *Dr. D.?* She waves frantically. "Stop."

Shoot, missed him.

A lock of hair falling in her face, she keeps an eye on his car. As he turns on Beacon, she steps into the next lane.

A stupid moment, and she feels air compress in the space between her body and a rapidly advancing, yet unseen, mass. Tires shriek. She tenses, biceps, fists, belly, thighs. Her eyelids clap shut, cheeks clenching, lips askew—impact imminent. *Too bad. I didn't think it would end like this. I'm not finished...*

Interminable seconds fill with honk-honk-honking, and a hot breath warms her legs. She levers open a reluctant eye. She pushes aside her hair.

Before her, headlights blazing, the silver grill of a red Mustang smiles wide and malevolent, the horn accelerating to a steady blare.

Affronted, Maggie faces the car. Her kneecaps at the bumper, she slams her palms on the hood. "Stop with the noise!" she yells at the middle-aged driver leaning over the steering wheel. His purple face close to the windshield, his mouth runs a stream of muffled words.

She frowns. "What?" she says, a hand behind one ear. The driver bounces in his seat. His head hits the ceiling, raising a black pimple in the convertible top.

She shrugs, palms up. He flips her another kind of bird.

Her eyebrows jack wrinkles to her hairline. She straightens. "In your dreams!" she screeches. Hank as her hero, she sticks out her tongue and stalks into the final lane of mercifully stopped traffic.

"Hey, lady." A young driver in the first car opens his door and leans over the top. "You need help?"

"Not me," she says. "He does." She points an accusing finger at the Mustang. Engine roaring, the Mustang, wheels spinning, leaves a trail of acrid smoke. *Some people!* Maggie salutes the Good Samaritan and marches into the Common's lower field.

Off the path, she eases out of her shoes. Her ankles feel hot and the cold ground is a relief. Through the dark trees, the lights of the buildings seem a long way off. She sits, legs extended wide, and wiggles her toes at the moon.

She rubs her ankles, fattening like the bedpost-biddy at the Ritz. *Another sign, but what?* She lies back, her feet facing uphill. "More rest, that's the ticket." She needs strength to get home, though strength hadn't worked in boarding school, that supposedly safe place where geometry and Latin were the least of her lessons. There, she learned the crush of dominance, the bitter edge of protection, the very things Clair, or The Home, would no doubt duplicate.

�❧

God, that first day as a boarder—

Maggie, in the role of Rapunzel, her long hair cut short for the occasion, ate her last breakfast at the farm's kitchen table: fried eggs from the henhouse, scrapple, *the best,* crisp and hot, her mother's homemade bread toasted golden. It all tasted like cardboard going down, and worse on the long car trip when it came back up.

Her new woolens itched. The Oxfords pinched.

Her black cat paced the hall where Maggie's suitcase awaited transport to the car. The cat rubbed and rubbed against the Samsonite, marking it better than a sewn-in tag.

"Dishes in the sink," her mother said. "Don't shilly-shally, we're late." Maggie dragged her bag to the car.

Halfway across Bucks County, breakfast reasserted itself. Once they hit the Schuylkill Expressway, they couldn't stop. "Too dangerous," Mother said, and Maggie leaned out the window.

On arrival at school, she slumped in the passenger seat, eyeing the heavy door of a once-grand house. Your room, the summer letter decreed, is on the top floor.

Resistance futile, Rapunzel trudged up two long flights of stairs toward the garret. When she flagged, Mother propelled her from behind. *Just as Clair will push me into The Home.* The stairwell smelled of disinfectant.

Halfway up the second flight, Maggie heard a cough. She lifted her head, and above her on the top step loomed Brunhilda Von Apenhausen, the resident overseer. Broad of beam and breast, her horns were no doubt hidden in the thick braids wound around her head.

Sweat soaked Maggie's shirt. Her saliva, dried to paste, stuck her tongue to the roof of her mouth.

The woman spoke to Maggie's mother in a hearty contralto, straight from the depths of her operatic lungs. The two women compared their origins and, arm in arm, bonded by the time Maggie entered her cell.

When her clothes hung in the closet, she opened the room's tiny window. *Too small to crawl through.* Long hair or no hair, escape was impossible.

Proclaiming her safe, Maggie's mother hurried down the stairs without so much as a backward glance. *Safe, that's what Clair says, too.*

Only Mother's hurry and the cracked voice gave her stress away, not that Maggie knew the signs until she had her own children, the love fierce, their happiness paramount.

Frau Von Apenhausen clapped her thick hands in front of her expanding breast. With an ecstatic smile, she said, "You so like my sweet Gretel looking," and gave Maggie's arm an appreciative pinch. Without Hansel to help her, being Rapunzel suddenly looked good.

In the garret, two other girls lived in separate cells, but Maggie garnered an *honor* beyond them. On account of the bond her mother had forged, Maggie reaped rewards she never intended to sow and certainly never mentioned to her mother.

"Lights out." Night after night for the week it took Maggie to learn to turn away, the widow Von Apenhousen leaned over her in the school's lumpy cot. With heavy breath looming closer, the woman patted Maggie's hair and planted a dry kiss on her forehead.

"We be such much friends," she said. "You and myself in this place."

It was the widow's first year too, but mutual terror didn't make them friends.

"It's just a year," her mother had said.

Just a year—Father working in London, and their farm, all animals including her cat, rented to strangers. But in less than two months, Mother flew back.

At the airport, she descended the rollaway stairs, in her hands a white box six-by- six-by-six inches. On the side, capital letters spelled Father's name and the day of his death.

Maggie never saw the farm again.

ଚଠ ଓଷ

Across the Boston Common field, a low tide perfume blows in. The ground seeps cold into Maggie's bones, and she slips Dan's wingtips back on. Following a path into the trees, she hunts for a bench, a place to sit and unfold her curling yellow stickies.

Almost to Tremont, *A bench, there*, safe behind bollards blocking taxis about to jump the curb. Protected, she curls happy as a cat, tucked into the fur of her coat. But her stomach talks, nothing to eat since tea, and her hair's driving her crazy. *In no time, I'll turn Rasta.*

It happened to that neighbor of Clair's—the cat, all mats. It had to be shaved.

A skinned rat named Fluffy. Maggie stifles a giggle. She shouldn't laugh, the mats were a misery for the poor thing, pulling the skin till it tore. *I won't wait for that.*

Maggie pats the knife in her pocket. *This should do.*

She sits up on the bench and spies a doughnut shop—*When I'm done, I'll go there.* She locks the knife open, pulls the last pin from her hair, and leaning forward flips long locks between her knees. The longest strands pool on the ground. She twists a fistful into a rope, and with the blade close to her scalp, she saws until her hair lies on the walk—no doubt, the making of some bird's future nest.

She riffles her finger-length coif, not a mat to be felt in the steely cowlicks. She's lighter, ready for anything. Hungry, and so conveniently, there's a Dunkin' on the corner.

I'm coming, Dunk.

CHAPTER 13

HANK

Wednesday Night

Back in his house, Hank's ear hurts. He'd like to pinch Mrs. G.

Ma grabs him. Shakes him. "What on earth?"

Not-so-Amazing Man hangs his head. "I had to find Nana."

"Oh, Hank." Ma hugs him. He feels a hitch in her breath, and the pistol in his jacket pocket jabs him. He squirms away. "We have to find her."

"Leave it to Uncle Rog and me." She holds Hank's arms, hers out stiff, and stares straight into his eyes. "I'm going now. Ben's in charge, so no foolishness."

"Yeah," Ben says from behind her. "'Cause I'll incinerate you."

Hank pats the pistol in his pocket. *Ha, not likely.*

For hours, Hank lies in bed, Zip curled beside him. Sleep comes and goes.

It's hard to know what to believe. Is Nana at the hospital, asleep in the best hiding place ever? Or out in the dark?

The dark scares Hank sometimes. It never scares Nana. He misses her. He misses Jeremy, too. He's more fun to play with than Ben or Sasha, but not as much as Nana.

Did bad guys get her?

His nose drips. He's *not* crying. Major Amazing Man doesn't. He wipes his nose on the pillow.

Zip sits up, ears at attention. He leaps off the bed, out the door, and down the stairs. A car door slams outside. Zip snuffles the front door. It creaks open.

"Shhh." Coming in from outside, Ma hushes Zip, and tiptoes up the stairs. All out of breath, she stands by Hank's bed.

"Did you find her?" he asks.

"Soon. In a few hours, Uncle Rog and I will go back out." She tucks in his blankets. He takes a shallow breath, heart beating fast, so afraid she'll stumble on the weapon he tucked under his mattress.

"You sleep," she says.

How can Hank sleep? He has to find Nana. Leaving it to Ma and Uncle R won't work. Uncle R is the Incredible Shrinking Man when it comes to bad guys. Guys like the one at the candy store.

※

Jeremy had promised Hank a bag of taffy, but coming out of the store, he and Uncle R teased each other. "I want pink," Jeremy said. "It's mine."

"No, I get the pink!" Uncle R jumped at the bag Jeremy held above his head.

People smiled and dodged their shenanigans—that's what Nana calls them.

"OK, but Hank first." They stopped in the middle of the sidewalk.

"Move it," said a nasty voice. Someone behind them hawked and spat.

Uncle Rog turned turtle, shoulders up around his ears. He walked away fast.

Not Jeremy. Jeremy held out his hand to the guy, a pink candy on his palm. "Want a taffy?"

"Not from you, faggot."

"You don't know what you're missing," he said. Then he shouted to Uncle R, "Wait up." He untwisted the pink candy, tossed it high, mouth open and snap, caught it. He chewed slowly on their way to Uncle R.

Catching up, Hank asked, "What's a faggot?"

"Well, it's…" Jeremy looked at Uncle Rog. Uncle Rog race-walked to the car.

※

Waiting for Ma to go to sleep, Hank counts five times to fifteen, then slides out of bed. He sneaks to the stairs, and halfway down he stops. Oh cripe—Ma and Uncle R are on the sofa, their coats on Clyde's chair. Hank watches through the spindles.

"Six hours and not a sign." Ma closes her eyes tight. Uncle R falls against her. His back shakes. Zip does that when he heaves up gross stuff at the beach.

"We'll find her, Rog." Sitting straight, Ma runs her hand on his back. "Don't cry." She wipes her own eyes.

Kicking off her sneakers, Ma strips her socks and wiggles her toes.

"Oooo, blisters, you'll need Band-Aids."

"We need more than Band-Aids," she says. "We need searchers. Pictures on lampposts."

"The police have an old one, Mum at the Gala. So elegant."

"And Jeremy, we need him. Did you call?"

"I can't." Uncle R screws up his face. "He's never coming back."

Ma slides close. He pulls away. "And we're never going to find Mum."

"What?" Hank claps a hand over his mouth.

"Hank!" Ma stands.

He bolts up the stairs, slams his door, and jumps under the covers. He snores loudly.

Ma comes in. He curls up, his back facing her. Blankets to his neck, he covers his cape, the mask out of sight under his chin.

"We're going to find her." She kisses his head, tiptoes to the door, and closes it behind her.

But how? What's their plan?

He gives her time to get to the sofa, and then follows. At the stairs, he drops to his knees. Slithers down on his stomach till the front room comes in view.

"… you can't blame Jeremy." Ma sits on the edge of the sofa. "You didn't want him—more fool you."

"I never said that." Uncle R picks at his thumbnail.

"What's wrong with you? You can't let anyone close, and it's not just Jeremy. Not me, and not Mum, either."

"That's not true, and I don't want to talk about it. Besides, what could I tell him? We don't know what's happened."

"You never talk. It's always about the homeless." She shoves his head, but not hard like Ben does to Hank. "*You* are homeless; why not take care of you? And Jeremy. He needs you."

Uncle R pulls away.

"You're so damn prickly, you drive people off."

"No, people leave." Uncle R looks in his lap. "Dad, Mum, everyone leaves except you, and you made me leave."

"You need to be with Jeremy," she says. "You love him, and he loves you."

Up off the sofa, Uncle R stomps in a circle. He shoves hands in his pockets. He chews the corner of his lip.

"What's the matter, Rog, afraid toads will jump out?"

He glares. "I don't want to be a faggot, OK? I don't want to look over my shoulder and wonder if some nutter's going to jump us."

He makes fists. "Every time Jeremy came in late, I saw him in a bloody heap." He falls back on the sofa. "I want a wife and kids. I want to be a family; something stable."

"Not like Rick and me, is that what you mean?"

Hank holds tight to the spindles. What *about* Ma and Dad?

"That's not—well, yes. It would tear me apart. Now Mum's tearing me apart."

Ma takes both his hands. "You'd rather not try?"

"I can't."

"Never see him again? You'd be fine with that?"

"His choice. He left."

This time Ma shoves him hard. "Sleep with him one minute, not the next? Jesus, Roger, and what about *that girl*?"

Uncle R groans. "I was jealous. He touched...."

"And you wanted revenge, what's wrong with you? A physical therapist touches people."

"I can't manage the want. Jeremy revels in it, and all I have is…" he presses his fingers on his forehead. "…is shame. And Mum made it worse."

"How? By accepting you?"

"She tries too hard, it always sounds like a lie, like you telling Hank we'll find Mum."

Hank knew it. It's up to him now.

"Anyway, I've blown the whole thing."

"What did you do, Rog?"

"You know *that girl*? She's…" Uncle Rog rests his hands on his belly. Ma does that when she has that woman thing.

"Jesus, Rog."

Uncle R says, "Talk about revenge, I bet Mum's hiding."

"Roger, she isn't who she was. Deal with it."

Hank scratches his ear on the spindle. If she isn't Nana, who is she?

Uncle R taps his head. "She knows exactly what's what."

"Either way, she's alone out there. It's dangerous." Ma shuts her mouth tight. Maybe *she's* afraid toads will jump out.

"Clair, do we *have* to do this?" Uncle R uses his begging voice. Ma looks up. "Do what?"

"Sell her house."

"Damn it." Her spit flies. "You know we do. The sale's on; and the Pines. If she won't come here, they'll take her."

"But we haven't closed."

"We're committed." She stabs his chest with a finger. "And you agreed."

"She'll hate it, the name alone—" He gags. "Your Home at Whispering Pines."

Ma pulls on her socks. "It's not Dickensian; and it's up to her: there or here."

"If we find her."

"We have to." Ma jams on her sneakers. "I'll call her neighbors; I'll call everyone we know."

Hank scoots backward up the stairs.

"It's three in the morning."

"I don't care what time it is." Hank hears her words fade toward the kitchen. "...that girl, pregnant or not, call Jeremy or I will."

CHAPTER 14

MAGGIE

Wednesday Night

Doughnuts make her think of sex—sex and doughnuts, two things considered inappropriate for young ladies. The doughy circles add an adipose layer to the hips and thighs, while sex can distend the belly. Before marriage, either would jeopardize the future, or so Mother claimed.

Maggie tightens the phone cord. Passing fingers through her spiked hair one more time, she crosses out of the park, glad she's not a young lady anymore.

Through the door of Double-D, conspicuous plenty assails her in the form of those sugary circles. There are banks of them, plus muffins and bagels and croissants, flat pastries, and fat, twisted thises and lots of thates. A counter-boy slouches in the midst.

"Whad-a-ya-wan?" he says without looking up from his navel. *Is this how Roger behaves, serving dinner to the homeless?*

"Well?" He looks up.

"Oh, good, you do speak English." She puts two fingers to her chin and frowns. "Ummmm…"

As a kid she had a choice of jelly, glazed, or plain. Now she's boggled by improbable slicks of colored icing, others topped with a sprinkle of chopped crayons. Others are sandwiches with sweets or sliced meats; salads wrapped in edible paper, and more combinations too appalling to consider.

And drinks. She can't identify Joe in a box, chai, latte, dunkaccino, or coolatta. Such toxic colors. Do people actually drink this stuff? *And aren't coolattas shorts?*

"Come on lady," the counter boy snaps.

Too flustered to ask what's what, she orders, "One raised-glazed, please."

"Drink?"

"Hot… hot…ch… chocolate." Thank heaven, she remembered the word.

"You wan-a-shot-in-at?"

"A what?"

He bangs his hands on the counter and yells, "A shot, a shot."

She draws up prim. "Certainly not, I don't do shots."

He slides her order onto the counter and holds out his hand. *Money.* She turns her back. Without opening the coat, she fishes down to her pocket and retrieves Mother's stash.

He breaks her Lincoln, gives her a Washington and three dirty pennies.

She holds the money flat on her palm. "That's all?" she asks.

He points at a list on the wall. "Read 'em an' weep, Gra'ma."

She ducks her head and carries her forbidden meal to the counter by the window, her eyes shifting away from the eyes of every passerby.

She lays the doughnut on its paper, the cocoa beside it. Turning the cup, she struggles with its plastic top. *Who puts a childproof cap on cocoa?*

She twists and pries. Steam rises from a tiny hole in the lid. She breathes it in, sweet and calming. Letting it cool, she bites slowly into the soft doughnut. So unlike the cakey ones Mother used to make, a cinnamon treat Maggie didn't care for.

Why was it, that what she didn't have always looked better? At school she traded a lamb sandwich on homemade wheat for Chuckey's bologna on Wonder Bread. Mother nearly killed her.

The sugary glaze sticks to her lips. Little pieces fall, and she bends over the paper. A shame to miss a single sliver. She dabs them with a licked finger.

How good the cocoa would be. She pries again. A geyser of dark shoots up through the little hole in the lid and onto the paper. "Oops."

A pudgy man on the next stool slides his pastry paper away from the encroaching puddle. She hadn't noticed him before.

If she had, she wouldn't have taken a second look. Not date material, not if she were forty, not sixty, not at a hundred and five. As if she's "looking," though she does like to look. Now she can. No need to worry if they'd take an interest; she's invisible.

Mr. Pudgy, beside her, flattens the paper down to its last wrinkle. He touches his elbow with two fingers, rubs the inside of his wrist, and pulls a hair-tufted lobe. With both hands, elbows out, he raises the doughnut to his mouth and bites, then lowers it to the exact center of the paper, the crescent bite facing six-o-clock. Maggie rolls her eyes.

Who is she to judge? She, who lines up plastic knives and forks on a hospital tray? *Maybe his treat tastes better this way.* He dabs a fallen sprinkle and places the red dot on his tongue.

Doesn't mean we're alike.

He sips his lidless coffee, clever enough to get at his drink, which is more than she can say for herself. Whatever his technique, it works.

She touches each elbow, rubs her wrist, and attacks her cup again. *Damn.*

"May I help?" he says, all serious, blue-eyed through thick glasses. He smooths the tips of his fingers against his thumb like a safecracker.

Though balding with a fringe of wisps, he has something of the little boy about him, looking like a cross between Friar Tuck and her mother's kindest man in Christendom, that man, a male incarnation of a fairy godmother.

Might this hybrid-man be Maggie's saving grace, the way her stepfather had been when opening the gate to a new and opulent life? Certainly, there's nothing threatening about this fellow in his rumpled blue jacket, Oxford shirt, and chinos worn soft as the man himself. He could be a poster-boy for low-T.

Maggie slides her cup next to his rainbow sprinkled treat. "A little help would be nice," she says.

Using all ten fingers, he deftly lifts the lid without a spill. She sips and smiles her thanks.

His eyes follow pigeons chasing a gull over the Boylston Subway Station. "I love the birds," he says. If this is a line, she's heard better. He blinks like a bird, and stretches his neck sideways.

But birds, being her favorite, and him, so pink-cheeked and earnest, she finds she can't resist another glance in his direction.

"Which do you like?" he asks.

"Pheasants," she says. "The ring-neck."

"They're fine birds." He adjusts his glasses. "The ring-neck prefers open fields, protects its mate," he says, head tilted. "He keeps watch perched in a tree, while she nests on the ground in dense cover."

His shy offering, taken straight from Audubon, captures her. "Do you walk in open fields?"

"Not much, I prefer the beach," he says. "But birds find me, all kinds."

"This morning," Maggie says, excitement on the rise, "I saw my favorite going to the park." Off her stool, she stands to her full six feet, arms out, showing how it flew.

She looks down at her coat, its inside-out silk above wide wingtips. If he looked like she does, she'd be afraid. What could he be thinking? *A bagless old bag, what else?*

"Shouldn't be here," he says.

"I have as much right as you." With a huff, she sits on her stool.

"I mean the pheasant. He doesn't live here. He's a vagrant."

Mollified, she takes another bite of her doughnut. The man reaches out his index finger and touches the stitching on her coat, sliding it along the script name. "Is that you, Laura?"

Maggie flinches. "No, my mother."

She hears Mother's voice, *Won't you introduce me? What does his father do? I don't think much of his...*

Muuutherrrr, we're eating doughnuts, not getting married.

"I'm Wilbur," he says, running a wrist under his moist nose.

"Call me Maggie," she says, and copying her mother, she asks, "What do you do?"

"I make do." He gives a slow smile. "You know, a Bridgewater talent."

"A nice town, is it? I've never been."

"Oh, I thought you were a graduate, too." He gives her a long head-to-toe appraisal, his forehead lined with confusion. "I didn't see the town 'til they sprung me. I wasn't sick enough to stay, not dangerous enough, so no locked ward." He smirks. "Freedom by government decree, but I'm fine now. And you?"

"I ran away." She pushes her sleeves above her elbows. "Seven dollars and three pennies to my name, a mink, and this doughnut." She takes the last in one big bite.

"Won't someone worry?"

She swallows and blows on her cocoa. "No, Bobby and I go camping all the time, Mother never minds. Besides I'm searching for a... L... L... lawyer."

"My sister wanted to be a lawyer," he says. "She's a worry." He swivels on his stool. "You look like her; it's the hair." He holds his hands above his head, fingers stiff in all directions. "Punked-out, the youngsters call it. You're right in style."

Maggie checks a reflection in the window. *His sister looks like that?*

His eyes wander into the treetops. "Punk wasn't in style then. God knows what she looks like now. I haven't seen her since Bridgewater." He scrubs his nose on a napkin and tucks it in his pocket. "I looked and looked, but no luck. I hope somebody nice found her." He wags a finger at Maggie. "You're too trusting—I told her. Would she listen? Not a bit. She knew best. A heart big as a house, and couldn't tell true love from a drugged haze."

Drugs—Maggie had forgotten the pills in her pocket. Should she take one, more than one? If she could get them out of her pocket. Wearing the coat inside out still has its disadvantages. And she certainly won't open it now.

Wilbur's finger reaches for her head, but he pulls short of touching. "Sis said I should rob a bank, twenty years free room and board." He rolls his shoulders. "Better than being homeless. But I'd miss my birds."

"Homeless?"

"Sort of." He sips his coffee.

"You don't look homeless."

He leans closer. "That's the trick, not to look it."

She barely hears him, what with the shop full of chatter. A hand plunks a cup on the counter, right where she'll spill it, and a man squeezes between her seat and Wilbur's.

"Let's go," says Wilbur. She looks mournfully at her cup.

"Bring it," he says. They climb off their stools, cups in hand, and leave into the yellowish night of Boylston St.

"Where will you go?" he asks.

She tips her head toward the Common, where black trees blot the blue-black sky and tiny lights snake paths into the depths. "That's where…

Shouting erupts, and laughter as a gaggle of hooligans, Mohawked and pierced in improbable places, jostles around them. Her lukewarm chocolate sloshes. She raises her arms, cup high. Someone steps on her toe. She trips. The drink soaks her sleeve.

All this jumping about, bad as Zip.

Elbows and arms knock her. Spin her. Hands roam her body. *Is this the airport?* Fingers invade folds and crevices. *Not mine, the coat.*

An elbow smacks her cheek. "OW, OW, OW." Her cup takes wing, and she grabs for it, then at her glasses hanging cockeyed from her nose. The moth in her chest skitters her ribs, its delicate wing-beats increasing.

The traffic lights blink green to yellow. Her shoes search for a flat purchase they can't find, and the sidewalk tips into view. Her knees wonder where her feet went. One foot slips off the sidewalk, bringing her down, a hard sit, her hands on cement next to her rump, grit beneath her palms, the pull of gum.

"Wilbur?" All she sees are knees, shins, and shoes scrambling in the gutter.

"Score," a boy shouts. "Pills." He stands above her, studs in his eyebrow reflecting the yellow streetlight. He waves bottles in both hands, and the group dashes into the Common.

Half in the street, Wilbur crouches beside her. "You alright?" She takes a breath, the air crisp and cool. A doughnut paper blows past.

She wiggles her outstretched legs, wingtip-toes up. "Never better," she says. She folds her legs, about to get to her feet. "Oh, no."

She dabs a brown puddle and sniffs her fingers. "I spilled my dark," she wails.

"Your money? Did they get your money?"

Her coat loose, she feels inside. "Gone," she says. "And my pills." Her wail not so frantic as over the loss of chocolate.

Wilbur lays his arm around her shoulder. "I quit pills, and look at me. I'm fine." He straightens her glasses, not quite straight. "Someone got you good," he says.

"Cracked a lens." The crack seems to be down his face.

A passer-by squats beside them. "I called the cops; they'll be here any second. Is she OK?"

"She's fine." Wilbur pulls her to her feet, a quick look up Tremont and down Boylston. "She lost her balance, is all. No need for police." He holds her close. She grips her coat, the cord about to drop. "Absolutely no need." With a protective arm, he guides her around the corner.

Something hard bumps her shin. Maybe a pill bottle fell through the pocket. She pats down by the hem. *Oh shoot.*

She jiggles the coat, sliding the lump to the side where it won't bang her shin as she walks. Saving her pills would've been better than the pistol. She braces against the corner building, her breath hard to catch, what with Mr. Moth scrabbling around.

"You don't look so good," says Wilbur.

"In a minute. The dizzies, they'll pass." She lists toward the wall.

"Sis got them, too." He tightens his arm around Maggie's waist. "Head between your knees might help."

She can't. Too hard to breathe. "Really, I'm fine now," she says. And she straightens, only to fall back to the wall.

He shakes his head, nods, and shakes it again. "Are you sure?"

But he isn't so much talking to Maggie. It seems like an argument with someone else.

"Not here," he says. "No, I can't leave her here."

Maggie's eye, where she caught the elbow, throbs. "Not here?" she asks.

"No, come with me," he says.

"With you!" Could he be her kindest man in Christendom? "With you where?"

"A secret," he says. "Homeless never tell."

Not even a first date and I'm... What would Mother say?

CHAPTER 15

MAGGIE

Still Wednesday Night, and Back in Time

Off Boylston, Maggie and Wilbur wend a maze of streets clogged with fumes. She coughs as they pass over a highway packed with post rush-hour trucks, their bumpers still kissing.

A cold wind gnaws her legs. Exhaustion rolls through her, a freighted train clacking her bones. She leans on Wilbur's arm.

Between Wilbur and her flying shoes, all would be well. She closes her eyes, her head on his shoulder, and he guides her.

₧⇛

She'd been homeless before.

"You're not out on the street," her mother had said. Yet that's how it felt, her father dead, and strangers renting her house. Money frozen.

She knew about hot money from movies, not something that happened to people she knew. But cold money? How did that work? That was the point, flash frozen, it didn't work.

Even if there'd been microwaves then, the money couldn't be thawed. No warm words with a banker would help, not even a hotheaded lawyer. "So sorry, Laura, the funds aren't yours. Wait for probate."

Maggie and her mother depended on the kindness of friends, a whole streetcar of desires unmet, but Blanche served as mentor while they hopped from garage apartment to mega-mansion to a converted storeroom, anyplace momentarily empty and offered. Their stays lasted from two days to two months, a year living out of suitcases, the time too short, or the space too limited to unpack.

Mother's wad of mad-money came into play. She stretched it, buying three-day-old bread, and her friend the butcher slipped her packets of liver wrapped in white paper, the liver in shades of green only a banker could envy.

Maggie, old enough and wise enough, wouldn't look a gift horse in the teeth, and still young enough, she trusted her mother to deliver a miracle.

The miracle—Mother sliced the slippery organs and dredged the chunks in wheat-germ. Fried crisp, Ketchup or not, it could have been steak.

ა୨ር෩

I could do with a bit of liver. A doughnut a day won't keep the doctor at bay.

"We'll be there soon," Wilbur says.

"Where?" she asks, as they cut into an alley and duck behind the prickle of evergreens.

"Watch it." Crouching low, he holds her hand and steps high. "See it?"

"See what?"

"Dental floss," he says, "Poor-man's alarm system."

Seeing nothing, she lifts her leg high, stealthy as a robber evading a laser beam, but invisible floss hits her shin, setting off a clatter of tin cans.

"Never mind," Wilbur says. "It's time to crawl." He pulls her to the ground.

Slow on all fours, she grunts. The last time she crawled in the dark, she'd followed Hank sneaking around the house, a secret from Clair. Only this time it's for real, truly needing not to be seen or heard.

I'd rather play sardines, it's less painful.

Crawling in a coat isn't easy. She tucks the tails into the cord at her waist, rubble biting her kneecaps. "Oo, oo." Wind balloons her johnny. Luckily, she's following Wilbur.

"What kind of home is this?" She wants to whine more, but curbs her tongue.

"Home for the homeless," he says. "Follow me."

A night in the Garden would have been easier. "I can't see." Her words jitter.

"Hold my foot," he says.

She knows this system from Hank. A firm grip on Wilbur's shoe, she lurches into the dark.

"Stay low, it's a small hole."

He's a sadist. What am I doing?

She eases slowly forward, neck bent. Feeling the touch of brick on one shoulder, she ducks lower, shifts, and hits the other one. *Small as a gopher hole.*

Under her knees, the surface goes soft, the smell of heat dry in her nose. "We're here," he says, his quiet words no longer lost in the great outdoors.

"Watch the curtain." A heavy cloth touches her head, slithers against her back, falling behind her feet. The breeze is shut out.

"Wait here." He keeps his voice low.

Warmth surrounds her bare legs and crawls up cozy under her coat, overshadowing the ache in her knees. She caresses the rubble's imprint on her skin and listens beyond her breath to a distant hum easily recognized as a well-tuned furnace.

Without a sound, soft lights fill an expanse of brick-walled tunnel, Maggie at the entrance, kneeling on a black shag rug. She takes in his home, snug as Benjamin Bunny's burrow, only people-sized with a bed, a kitchen-like section, and a red beanbag chair. Wilbur twists two more bulbs hanging from a black cord running along the ceiling.

He ducks his head at the lowest of many pipes, and folding his jacket, he places it on a shelf at the end of a mattress. The bed has been set on a Styrofoam slab and pushed long-ways to the far wall, the brick covered with bright colored blankets. Many pillows against the wall make the bed inviting as a sofa. He smooths the blue spread.

"Welcome," he says continuing to whisper. "It's not much, but it's home."

With relief to her knees, she stands, her head just missing bundles of wires, red, blue, green, and white, strung beside the pipes. Past the beanbag chair, they disappear in a dark tunnel.

"Have a seat," he says offering the sofa. "Dining room, living room, bedroom in one, we'll have to share." Hangdog shy, he tips his head. "I'll keep to my side, pinkie-swear."

If she can sleep in a bed with Zip, she can sleep beside Wilbur. A positive palace compared to a night in the park. Funny how perceptions change.

She walks across a patchwork of carpet, the squares softening the cement, and eases herself onto the mattress. Her back rests against the pillows, feet out over the edge like a little kid in a big chair.

"We have to be quiet." He points at the wood ceiling. "They'll call an exterminator, or worse, the police, and poof, all gone."

"Who…"

Overhead, little steps drum louder and louder. Bigger feet pound after. A door slams.

"Number one," says a deep voice from above. "You did it, yay."

"I get a chocolate kiss," this from a high-voiced child. "Right?"

A sudden gush sounds down a fat pipe on the wall. Maggie expects a flood on the floor.

"Just flushing," says Wilbur. "Three apartments. Soon you won't notice."

Chocolate after peeing, a good plan. "All this running water makes me… where is…" Maggie crosses her legs.

Wilbur's ears turn pink. "The facilities," he clears his throat, "are behind the curtain." He scoots to the end of the lighted space and folds back a cloth showing a small area with hooks on the wall, and on the floor a box topped with an oak toilet seat. The box, open on one side, houses a fine china pot, big-bellied with painted flowers and a turned lip.

With some trepidation, she ducks behind the curtain. She sniffs, all set to be revolted, but the air is fresh, and not the fresh of freshener, either. If cleanliness is next to godliness, Wilbur is one godly man.

Returning to the main room, she holds the mink over one arm while clutching the johnny closed behind her. "All the comforts of home, including antiques," she says. "A huge improvement over the Common's porta-pisser."

"I find what I need." He shifts his gaze from her thighs, so clearly on display. "Looks like you need a shopping trip— Goodwill tomorrow?"

"My money." Facing him, she pats her coat pockets. "Where's my money?"

"They didn't get mine," he says. "And I worked today. That's why the fancy duds." He retreats behind the curtain. She hears his shoes drop and the click of his belt buckle.

"Getting comfy," he says. "I'll be right out."

Returning, more boyish than ever in panda pajamas, he folds the good clothes. At the foot of the bed, he places them on top of zip-lock bags. Maggie gives him a questioning look.

"Temp-work means clean clothes," he says. "Clean go in Ziplocks, day-old on top. Panhandler's on the floor." Those are the clothes she expected of the homeless.

"It's a job. Lots of money, if you know where to stand and when." He straightens the stack of clothes. "You've got to know the ropes."

Near the head of the bed is another set of shelves topped with sea glass and stones in little piles, the glass organized by color, milk of magnesia blue, plain milky, and wine bottle green. Granite stones, no bigger than speckled bird eggs, nest together in varying sizes from ostrich to hummingbird.

"My collections," he says as she roams, examining every surface. Here, small cars. There, frogs and lizards and superheroes in unlikely poses.

The tallest shelves mark off a Pullman-like kitchen with a camp stove, a pitcher with four fingers of water in the bottom, and no sink for more.

"How about a drink?"

"No thanks," she says. "I'm fine."

Wilbur sips from the pitcher, and opens a circle in the wall. He lights a flame on the stove. "You want soup?" he says and takes two cans from an extensive row: clam chowder, minestrone, tomato, gumbo. Without waiting for an answer, he cranks open two gumbos and throws the opener back in a box alongside one fork, a spoon, and a knife.

A shelf below the cans holds books: Dan Brown, Sue Grafton, Billy Collins, Stephen King, and below them, bottles of Kaopectate. "You do take medicine."

"When pizza's too long in the dumpster, I do." He stirs the gumbo, the aroma drawing her to the stove. Maggie salivates. Her stomach clamors in anticipation.

"There's a pizzeria," he says, "where they toss a pie if it sits more than twenty minutes." He spoons thick stew into a bowl. "The pizza's hotter than delivery, not that I get delivery." He hands her the only bowl along with the spoon, and a hard roll. "If you dip it..."

"Can't tell it from fresh," she says.

"You know stale bread?"

"A short stint, but it sticks with me."

He drinks from the pan, his eyes smiling over the rim. "I've never hosted dinner."

Dinner with Wilbur had no silver or candles, yet it couldn't be beat.

"It's the best ever," she says. And it is.

80 03

Maggie's first meal with polished silver and candelabras came close on the heels of green liver. Bernard Helmsworth made it happen. Introduced by a friend, he came to the house where Bobby, Maggie, and their mother lived that month in the basement.

He should have come accompanied by fanfare and heralds as befit a shimmering knight, but no, this balding, male incarnation of Cinderella's fairy godmother came without fanfare or glitter, came without pumpkins or rats, and made magic without waving a wand.

Mother forbad his use of the wand harbored behind his zipper. "Not 'til after the wedding," she told him. Yet his loving eyes stayed set on Mother, his shy deference winning Bobby and Maggie when he asked their permission before bending his knee.

Mother allowed that it all seemed so fast. But a yes was given.

Her answer brought on the vetting at Sunday dinner, the three of them under the scrutinizing eyes of Bernard's extended family massed in the great hall of a seaside house. A footman (was he?) offered glasses of brown liquid—Shooting Sherry, he called it—a last drink before execution? Maggie declined.

Milling together, aunts gave uncles side-long glances. The step-sibs-to-be nudged cousins. Slitty-eyed, they picked at the crown of her drooping pageboy, then descended to the hem of the wrinkled dress she'd ironed twice. In the midst of it all, an aging gorgon (the grand-gorgoness) reigned tall and aloof. Down the slope of her nose, the creature surveyed Maggie, no doubt catching a hint of the dungarees and manure-soaked boots she'd replaced with itchy stockings and too tight flats that bound her toes in growing complaint.

When seated in the dining room, she gratefully slipped the shoes, half-bare heels hidden beneath her chair, and tucked herself close to the damask-covered table. Mother sat at the opposite end with Bobby, too distant to offer protection against the gorgon (on her right), gray hair coifed stiff as the spine Maggie held three inches off the back of her chair.

Where to look? She wrung her fingers. What to say to the gorgon or the gorgonettes, the two sitting across the table?

Looking past their heads, Maggie's eyes followed a fly to the sideboard. It cruised open sherry bottles. She'd rather talk to the fly than the steps. What with Maggie being akin to Cinderella, the sibs must be Anastasia and Drusilla.

The fly looped from the sideboard, over the table to Anastasia's empty sherry, and *snap*, she grabbed it. She squeeeezed, then released one finger at a time, and on her palm displayed broken wings cocked at an angle, six legs twitching from the center of the fly's oozing thorax. Drusilla grinned.

Maggie winced and studied the array of long-stemmed glasses, gleaming knives, and various spoons and forks at her place. These and a giant plate bode well for the plenty to come, but no serving dishes sat in the center of the table, only her own tiny saucers of salt and pepper with their own itty-bitty spoons.

The Gorgon stomped her foot under the table.

Panic. Had the gorgon smelled Maggie's half-eased feet?

The door to the kitchen whomped open and then swung shut again behind a woman dressed in black with a white apron. She snatched Maggie's plate.

No dinner? Blinking back tears, she shoved her toes fully into their bindings. The door whomped again, and another woman gave her a smaller plate. Phew, punishment downgraded.

"Fish, Miss?" said a voice at her ear. She lurched, and a gasp went around the table as the platter with a whole skinned salmon wobbled above her head.

The server lowered the dish closer to her arm. Hmmm—does the first to be served take the head? The tail? Digging into the middle seemed rude.

The cloudy-eyed fish gave no hint. Anastasia snickered.

OK. The tail. She dug with a wide fork, and the whole fish swam to the edge of the platter. Stopping the slide, she discovered hidden cuts in the middle, and lifted out a small piece.

To make the portion last, she took tiny bites with the smallest fork. The gorgon gave a tight-lipped smile.

Maggie spied more fish languishing on the sideboard. "Would you like seconds?" said the grand-gorgon with a slight arch of an eyebrow.

Maggie nodded. On the farm, she'd eaten what she caught, catfish and eel.

"Help yourself."

She loaded the gold-edged plate. No one else took more, all waiting, hands folded as she rushed the last forkfuls.

Another stomp on the floor brought two ladies. One cleared. One brought larger plates. Dessert! Baked Alaska the size of the state?

Instead, came a whole spread-eagled bird, skinny beans with almonds, a twice-stuffed potato—dinner again!

Raised to clean her plate, she did. Twice-stuffed, her sympathies to the potato.

And more after that—a plate with a bowl of clear soup sat on a circle of lace. Lemon slices floated on top.

The hint of a splash from the gorgon's direction stopped Maggie's reach for a spoon. The oh-so-proper gorgon, hands above her bowl, twiddled fingers in the soup. Around the table, everyone twiddled. Was this a case of *The Emperor's New Clothes?* Bobby guffawed at the opposite end of the table. Maggie's face grew red to the roots of her hair.

That bowl set aside, her fingers dried, another bowl appeared, full of yellow custard, a white blob in the middle.

"Mmm, floating island," said Drusilla.

Spoon high, Maggie watched another fly arc in sherry-induced circles. It hovered overhead, then dropped, a six-point landing on her sticky island. He pulled one leg free, the others sinking deeper. Wings buzzed. She squirmed in her seat. Bernard, all of a sudden beside her, leaned over her shoulder. "Shhh," he whispered with a sly grin and slid a spoon under the fly. "The others will want one." An old joke she hadn't heard before. He set the fly gently on the edge of the Gorgon's plate, a secret the three of them shared. Happily, Maggie tucked into the floating island.

₭₮

In Wilbur's tunnel, lights out and wrapped safe in mink, Maggie lies in his bed. She curls on her side, her back to the back of Wilbur's legs, the two of them head to toe.

She knew the method from Charlie's grandparents. If only she had a chocolate factory handy, this would be a mighty fine life.

A gentleman, her Wilbur, he offered her the outside edge, and she accepted without a qualm. Rolling out wouldn't be a problem, with only a five-inch fall to the floor.

She asks into the dark, "Did you always live here? After Bridgewater?"

"I tried missions," he says. "They seemed welcoming." He pauses so long she thinks he's fallen asleep.

"All those earnest young faces." He sits up and squirrels around. "They kept us company no matter how unwashed we were.

"Nice, I thought, them braving our bourbon-laced nonsense." He stretches his legs. "But soon they'd sit too close, their talk insistent. I could feel them dig into my brain first, then my heart, pressing in seeds they'd water and water with words until I lost my appetite." Breathing hard, he flops on his back, head at the same end as hers.

"They wanted me more than I wanted food and a bed. I can't understand why their good works hinged on my belief." He rolls again, switching so he faces her back, his gumbo breath swirling around her head. "Good works should stand on their own, shouldn't they?"

Another toss, and he hikes himself onto all fours. "Now I'm upset." The mattress shifts. A hollow at her back, she starts to roll and grips the edge.

She feels his weight against her, and with a grunt, he's on top, straddling her upper-most thigh. He plants one hand flat on the mattress behind her, the other in front.

The mattress gives as his weight shifts, rolling her to her back, and he's on her, her breasts flattened. Squirming, his body presses where it shouldn't, his breath hot in her face.

Oh Lordy. Her heart thunders up her throat.

Her fingers frozen in claws, she clutches the wrinkling sheet beneath her.

What happened to Mr. Low-T?

CHAPTER 16

MAGGIE

Wednesday Night into Tuesday Morning

Wilbur's panda PJs should have warned her. Pandas look so cuddly and cute, when in reality they're ferocious.

Fight. She's got to fight.

Or is it "don't fight, it's not worth your life?"

Scream. Yes, scream bloody God-damn murder. With a tinkling toddler in the house, they can't be heavy sleepers. *Scream.*

Under the grind of his shifting weight, a deep breath is near impossible. She drags at one, inflating her lungs as best she can, but before she finds her voice, his wispy hair brushes her nose. "Sorry," he grunts, "Sorry to crush you." And he rolls, in one smooth motion, onto the floor.

Her sightless eyes bug in the dark. She hears him shuffle into slippers, and cross the room. The lights come on. Her thundering heart beats a slow retreat down her gullet.

How else would he get out of bed? He wasn't going to levitate. He had to climb over.

"I've got to read or I'll blow my stack," he whispers. Hands above his head, he unscrews the two closest bulbs. At the far end, in a cone of light, he scooches into the red beanbag, pulls up his knees, and rests a book on panda-covered thighs.

Opening the slim volume, he says, "Billy Collins relaxes me, especially *Sailing Alone Around the Room*." He wiggles deeper into the beanbag and riffles the pages.

Silent for a bit, then out loud, he says, "Ah, 'Osso Buco,' listen to this, '...the sound of the bone against the plate ... me in a moat of risotto, ...'" He laughs and continues to himself, then sniffles. Is he crying? Billy makes Maggie do both.

With the bed hysteria settled, and head to toe again, Wilbur snoring, nothing stands between her and a good night's sleep.

Except, I'm parched. Her tongue sticks to furry teeth. Furry mink is one thing, but on teeth…

The gumbo did it, so salty, turning her mouth to a desert. *A drink.* What she wouldn't give.

Water gushes. If someone upstairs can find a dark bathroom, so can she. She rolls onto the floor. It's easier getting up from all fours on a hard surface. But once up in this sightless ocean, she can't tell which way she's facing. She paws the dark.

So, this is blindness. Nothing to touch, she tick-tocks foot to foot, turning in place. She wobbles.

Her legs spread for a wider base, and she bends her knees. The carpet squares feel wavy underfoot. She curls her toes, gripping the pile, arms out, balance precarious as if walking a tightrope.

She swats at the dark, stepping right, then left. There's nothing. She sees herself floating untethered in limitless space.

A ship, A ship, my kingdom for a ship. And so saying, her knee bangs into something hard. Like a drowning swimmer she hugs it, wood against her arms. Little bits clink under her hands. *Sea glass.* And now she's patting along the rocky shore of some dark ocean, fingering unrecognizable flotsam and jetsam.

Pictures take shape in her head: shelves, a table, the handle of a pot. Recognizing the terrain, she keeps one hand anchored, the other outstretched, waving for obstacles. *Worse than fog.*

Water gushes again and, *oh right,* this is the only running water. There is no sink, no real kitchen or bathroom. Like a mirage, the water pitcher comes clear in her mind where it sits next to the camp stove. She pats along the shelves, afraid of knocking over the pitcher. No, her biggest fear is that the thing will be empty.

She lifts her right hand high and brings it straight down. Her palm lands on the stove, clattering the metal stand. More to the left, high again, and down; *yes,* she touches the edge of the pitcher. Using both hands, she tips it to her lips, and swallows.

After two more delicious swallows, *even better than gin*, she taps her way back to bed. A nicer bed than the futon at Clair's. And no Zip.

Sleep is what she needs for tomorrow. It's a big day. She has to…to what? *God damn it.* Do what? It's nowhere near the tip of her tongue.

CHAPTER 17

CLAIR

Thursday

Clair stretches on her bed, eyes wide in the predawn-dark. Wrung out after hours of searching up Grove Street, over Revere, Anderson to Pinckney to West Cedar, climbing Mt. Vernon, down Joy. Down down down Joy, checking alleys, peering into gardens, stepping into dark stairwells. She wishes she believed in a god that would guide her to Mum, huddled in a state of... Clair snuffs the picture.

And worse than her imaginings, dreams rattle her. Lurid details jolt her from sleep. She lies there, muscles a-twitch. She beats her pillow. If they can't find Mum, how can there ever be peace? Without resolution, the end remains open, her imaginings bringing on nausea.

Out of bed, craving normalcy, she climbs the stairs to the third floor. Seeing her children asleep will calm her.

The door to Sasha's room stands ajar. She still likes the hall light on, quelling shadows, discouraging those things that could lurk under her bed. Her budding chest doesn't mean she's all grown up.

The light falls across her bed. Sasha's arm covers her face, the other around Fuzzy, the stuffed creature so threadbare his innards seep. Loved to pieces, one eye missing, he's no longer identifiable. Clair envies the ongoing comfort Sasha finds.

Ben never needed that stuffed animal love. He didn't stay still long enough, and when he did, he slept.

On to his room, she pushes against the chair blocking the door. Ben hasn't learned the trick of propping its back under the handle. Soon enough.

Spread-eagle, he snores like his father, arms and legs off the edges of the bed. Comfort is his by right, and he takes it.

Clair hesitates. He's all about close-held secrets, and she won't imagine them, not tonight. The driving lessons she promised worry her enough. This prowl through her children's bedrooms is supposed to be calming.

For now, he's safe in bed, too in love with his hockey stick to think about drugs. Rock and roll, yes. Sex? Mum is the one with her mind running to sex. Clair's sex life, and her precarious marriage. Right now, Rick is the least of her worries.

Hank next. Before she opens the door, she hears the squeak of the wheel as one of his mice runs. That wheel never stops. She is one with the mouse, and the squeak echoes in her chest.

If only Clair could talk to Mum. Are you in pain? The smallest disruptions always set her off.

Clair should have been more vigilant, made the move months ago. How could Mum be anything but terrified? Cold, hungry, at the mercy of... Right now, she could be... Clair covers her face with her hands. Stop this.

Steadying herself on Hank's headboard, she leans over him, catches a whiff of that little boy scent mixed with the smell of cedar chips and mouse urine. The cages need a change. She needs a change. Mum too, and yet everything's changing faster than Clair can grasp.

Focus. She's here for Hank. Amazing Man bound up in his mask and cape. He mumbles in his sleep, hair jutting eerily through the eyeholes. She eases the mask off his head, and sets it on the bedside table. True, he's not Superman, who only flies in the sky. He's more. Ever-entertaining, Amazing Man flies under water, through space and time, invisible to the naked eye.

Do eyes *ever* wear clothes—she loves his questions. Loves his world, one she wants to know, to hold, but can't in the hurly-burly she'd like to blame on Rick. He has many faults, but no, this is on her.

Still, Rick shouldn't belittle him. Hank isn't "too old," for costumes, and it's not "foolishness."

He used to encourage Hank, even made himself a matching cape, Major Amazing Man and Sargent Almost as Amazing,

Rick at his most lovable. The Rick she was sure would get better and better with age, a fine wine she sipped with such pleasure. How could a good wine turn, or had it been her poor pallet, too unsophisticated to taste the truth? That's worry for another day.

For this minute, the worry is Hank and his costume. He's not supposed to wear the outfit to bed. It could strangle him, yet Clair can't take it away, not tonight. He's more attached than Sasha to Fuzzy. Clair would have to amputate.

She unties the cape at his throat and watches him sleep, every twitch another concern. At least he's here, a sweet moment of peace calming her jitters.

But there can't be peace, not with Mum out there.

How does Roger keep it together? Oh right, denial.

He may as well be Clair's oldest child, downstairs rotting his brain in front of the TV.

He needs rest. His eyes look like they sting as much as hers.

She'll join him. Maybe his programs will bore her to sleep.

"What are you watching?" She cozies beside him on the sofa, careful not to slip into Zip's expanding pit. She really should make repairs. But Hank loves it.

"Damn it!" Roger snaps off the TV. "What possessed her?" Twisting, he faces Clair. "One minute Mum's fine, the next she's a stranger. Mothers aren't supposed to do that." He pounds both knees with his fists. "How could she do this?"

He pounds like Hank. It's all Clair can do not to laugh, but it's nice to know, under her jitters that she could still laugh. "You know, Mum didn't do it on purpose."

"Sometimes I want to smack her."

Clair takes his hands. "You'd never."

He pulls his hands away. "I've watched myself yell. So wrong, yet I kept spilling." He blinks back tears. "It's the same as hitting. I hate myself." He takes a red bandana from his pocket and blows his nose. "Jeremy and Mum, they're like best friends. No matter how outrageous she gets, he rolls with it."

"Could you perhaps be the least bit jealous?"

"OK, Ms. Psychobabble, tell me?"

"See, now you're attacking me." She moves to the other side of Zip's pit, knees up. "I never claimed to have it together. And yes, we both wish we could be easy as Jeremy. He lets everyone go at their own pace."

"Sure, until it's not *his* pace." Roger crosses his arms as if he has a right to be indignant.

"Jeremy is Mum's friend." Clair uncurls. Her feet drop to the floor. "And *we* better get used to being her parents."

"She's my mother." Roger retreats into the other corner of the sofa, his arms crossed tight. "I don't want to be a parent."

"But you've walked right into it, haven't you? Before, you were just a middle-aged adolescent, and now you're about to have a child, and not just a geriatric one."

"Not yet. She's not sure she'll keep it."

"A child, your child, and you're leaving the decision to that girl? Why—so you can say, 'Gee, Jeremy, I have to marry her.' And you haven't told her about him, have you?"

"She has no idea."

"When it comes to Jeremy, you look like a cock teaser. Now I see you're just self-centered. If you can't join Jeremy searching, go back to Curry House, play the Good Samaritan. They'll believe you."

CHAPTER 18

MAGGIE

Thursday

Maggie rises from a low bed. Her knees creak. Slivers of light slant from high on the wall of a dim brick tunnel. *Hell's bells! Where am I?* She blinks to clear her blurry eye. "Ouch." She touches it gently. It feels big.

"You OK?" A man pops up in the bed beside her. She retreats in one giant step. "Who…" She's heard of girls so drunk they wake up with a stranger. She'd never been that drunk. Surely, she'd have a giant headache. Wouldn't she be nauseous? *Well, my head does ache.*

The man throws off his covers and turns on the lights. "Shopping today," he announces. He stretches and scratches his belly.

She catches a name as it flies by. *Wilbur.*

"That eye," he says. "What a shiner."

Slowly, the where and the what come crawling back.

She retrieves her coat from the floor at the end of the mattress, and puts it on. Exercising the chamber pot comes next. She crosses to the curtain.

She squats onto the box with a thud. It's lower than she remembers. What with her morning creakies, getting up is a trick. It feels like her knees are high as her nose.

All finished, and no handle to grab, she can't lean forward enough to rise.

"You OK in there?" asks Wilbur.

"Fine, fine," she says and throws her weight forward, arms outstretched. The box wobbles. *Don't spill it.*

She tests the curtain. No, too weak, it's on a string.

"Sure you're OK?" His words sound urgent.

"Well…" She can't sit here all day, and he sounds worried.

Pretend he's an orderly. "I could use a hand, but close your eyes."

"Will do." He pulls open the curtain, eyes closed.

"All the way closed," she says, and he holds out his hands. She takes both.

"Around the wrists," he commands and braces. Latching on, he pulls. And up she comes, coat and johnny keeping her modesty.

"My turn," he says and disappears behind the curtain. After a long pause he sighs. "I'm shy this morning. No running water, so could you sing? Softly."

Without hesitation, she starts in, "Oh holy night, the stars…"

"Not helping."

"A jaunty one?" she says. "When I was one, I sucked my thumb, the day I set to sea…"

"I said softly."

She continues more quietly, "I climbed aboard a pirate ship, and the captain said to me, we go this way, that way…," and making up for the quiet she goes wildly forward and back, "over the Irish sea, a bottle of rum," she tips up a nonexistent bottle and rubs her stomach, "…to sooth my tum and that's the life for me. Yo-ho—When I was…," she raises two fingers.

"Thanks, I'm all set," Wilbur calls from behind the curtain.

Maggie continues, "…two, I…"

"No, stop, please."

"But…" She continues singing under her breath.

Out from behind the curtain, he tucks in his shirt and buckles his belt. "Well, I'm ready for breakfast." He reaches for the water pitcher and stops. Bending, he retrieves stones and sea glass from the floor. "Rats again, messing up my collections." He lines the pieces on the shelf, adjusting the order, *Down to a hundredth of an inch.* Finally done, he ducks outside with the water pitcher and reappears minutes later.

"A drink?" he asks. She looks around for a glass.

"I'll take the left side," he says. "You drink from the right." And they do.

Next, he opens a giant yellow box of Sugar Pops and takes a handful. He offers the wide wax paper opening. "On one condition: that you don't sing."

"Mmmm, Pops" she says taking a rubbery handful. "Rog and Clair's special- occasion cereal." The pirate tune worms ear-to-brain, and probably will all day. Still standing, she holds the Pops on the palm of her hand and nibbles the way a horse would.

"Don't bolt your food," he says before reclining on the bed as if he's a Roman emperor. He crosses his legs, and drops a little yellow nugget into his mouth. He chews with slow intent. "You've got to taste each one." He rolls the next one around on his tongue.

"A connoisseur of sugary confections?"

"Mostly, I know what I like, and I make it last." He drops in another. "Every little pleasure counts. Add 'em up and what do you get?"

Maggie reclines on the pillows at the opposite end of the bed, legs stretched, her feet against his hip. "What DO you get?" She opens her mouth wide and drops in a Pop.

"You get happy." He nudges her leg with his knee.

She tongues the Pop. Its lack of crispness no longer counts, and sweetness takes the moment. With careful chewing, it's almost the consistency of crème brulee. And crème brulee makes her happy.

Their breakfast cleanup makes her happier still. After three handfuls dropped in one at a time, she brushes her hands together, licks the tips of her fingers, and done. None of the hazards of Clair's kitchen, where a pleasant meal can easily go awry.

Hmmmm, Clair and Wilbur? Thoughtful as he is, Wilbur isn't right for Clair either, too close to Maggie's age. She best keep-on keeping an eye out.

But those worries are behind her. She lives here now. *Forget worries.* Maggie's good at forgetting.

High on song and a sugar rush, she creeps after Wilbur through the tunnel's entrance. "God, that's hard on the knees."

"Wait," Wilbur says. With his hands, he sweeps rubble aside.

"Much better." *Though not entirely comfy.* Nothing on the knees is these days.

On standing, Maggie finds herself in what must be a bombsite: a block's worth of yards full of demolished brick, cement clumps, broken timbers, and twisted fire escapes laced with stunted bushes and leggy ailanthus trees.

"What happened here?" she asks.

"Restoration through destruction." Wilbur sneers. He dips a tin cup in an oil drum lined with a tarp. "Our water supply." He drinks. "Tonight's your turn to wash the dish."

"Where are the workers?" she says.

"Developer ran out of money; everything stopped. It's a blessing for me." He brushes rubble back across the entrance, hiding their activity. "The man upstairs wants to sue. His wife wants to move. I hear every word." He claps dirt off his hands. "Come on, we better get going, but keep close to the wall."

Down the block and out of the rubble, they step to the sidewalk's smooth relief.

Going to Goodwill, Wilbur checks donation boxes. "People leave stuff on the ground, free for the taking."

"Nothing here," he says. "Shall we wash at Gulf or the Shell?" He nods farther down the block. "Gulf has hot water and blow driers. Shell has soap and brown paper towels. Take your choice."

"That's a choice?" Maggie looks at her dirty hands.

"Would you rather an outside shower?" Wilbur grins. "Hardly anyone looks."

"Don't tease." Maggie's too gritty for teasing.

"No really, this afternoon. Sun-warmed, the water's in a rubber bladder."

"Mmm, for now, the Shell." At least no more chalky hands.

After a cold wipe-down under her johnny, they continue to Harrison Ave., Goodwill's flagship in the distance. They walk in the wide gate past the intake truck, an eight-wheeled semi forlorn without its cab. A man, high in the back of the open trailer accepts armloads from a woman emptying the trunk of her car. A pickup pulls in beside her, and by the time Maggie and Wilbur reach the store, there's a line forming.

Inside, an ocean of clothes stretches to the horizon. Racks and racks in waves of reds and yellows, one rack all blues, another of greens from the deepest sea to the weakest tea. She swims, unable to focus, or even to think of what she might use or where to start looking.

High above, a smiley sign reads "Women": big letters emblazoned on red. *That's me.* She ducks under a rack of men's pants, browns and browns, and into the aisle of dresses.

When it came to shopping, maybe Mother had a point. In Boston, where she shopped, a personable young lady modeled one item at a time. It appeared ridiculous then. How could Mother know what the dress would look like on Maggie?

In schlumpy adolescence, her frame bore no resemblance to the wasp-waisted, colt-legged anorexic strutting before them.

Maggie still hates shopping, though a change from the johnny would be an improvement. She fingers her way down one rack. Wilbur drops a wide-brimmed hat on her head. "Fetching," he says. "We'll definitely get this. You can wear it to dinner."

"One dinner and you're Mr. Martha Stewart?"

He holds up a dress. "Try this."

She strips off her mink, and the johnny slips down one shoulder before he hisses, "No." Behind her, his hands on her elbows, he steers her to a dressing room no bigger than a phone booth. Who was it that always changed in a phone booth, emerging a different person? A powerful person.

While she changes, Wilbur passes her a chiffon gown, then drops boots on the floor. "Even if you're Martha Stewart, winter's hell, and wingtips won't do."

She emerges from behind the curtain, extending one leg first, long, slightly hairy above her new combat boot, laces undone. "To hell with Martha," she says. "I'm Gypsy Rose Lee." Hat at a slant, she vamps to the mirror. A gypsy-jolt looks at her.

She flips off the hat. A crop of gray hair shoots up all over her head, only hints left of her mother's haggard face with bent glasses. They tip sideways on her nose. Behind a cracked lens, her eye peers from under a swollen lid, the surrounding skin purple as a sunset moving toward black.

She shuns the mirror and attacks the seventeen buttons descending from her boney décolletage. She scrooches, itchy inside the dress.

"You've got it backwards," Wilbur says. "See, it pokes out here." He stabs a finger in her back. "That's where your titties belong, not shoulder blades."

Sleeping together, *and I mean sleeping,* seems to have made him less reticent.

She glances over her shoulder. "My witchy tits won't fly that high. I'd need a personal attendant with a pulley."

"That's what your kids want, an attendant?"

"Phooey," she says and catches his hand. "Let's see what else we can find, sweatpants, maybe." Her knees still smart. "Kneepads."

Her shoelaces drag as she walks the aisle. Household goods catch her eye. "We could use silver."

"A bowl or two might be nice, and a glass."

"Oh, Wilbur." Maggie holds up a bowl with a yellow rim, a fruit pattern in the bottom. "These are just like mine. And look, a whole set. Creamer and sugar, everything. They're rare. Only ten dollars, what a bargain."

"Yes," says a woman pushing Maggie out of the way. "And they're mine now."

"Don't fret, Maggie. We couldn't use so many, much less carry them."

"How about candlesticks? I love the gnomes." Something about them makes her stomach sink.

"We don't need candlesticks."

"And look here." She drags Wilbur down the row of tables. "Oooh, tools."

"You're looking for sweatpants. See, over there, a whole row."

Racks of them, dishwater-dyed in fifty shades of drab. She idly pushes hangers one to the next, and finally a purplish pair. Royal would be good, even papal, but no, this is a bruising purple.

She loosens the pair from the others, and along with it comes a slinky swirling blast of color, as if the whole store-full of color had been shrunk and hung on one plastic hanger. Holding it up, she shakes it before clasping the full-body suit against her front. She dances in a circle. The legs hang to her knees, one arm flopping short over her shoulder.

"Child size," says Wilbur. "What a shame."

"I'll try it."

"Don't be silly." He takes hold of the suit. "Here, I'll put it back."

Maggie keeps a firm grip. The suit stretches. "Oooh, hey." She checks the tag through cracked glasses. "It's spandex."

Wilbur raises his hands in surrender, and Maggie hustles to the changing booth.

Out of her boots, she stands skinny and wrinkled. She examines the floppy suit.

Propping an elbow against the wall, she balances on one leg, points her toes, and inserts a foot in the first leg. Pulling while standing one-legged isn't so easy. She tries to slide the other foot in, *Not the same hole,* and pokes about for the opening.

With two feet on the floor, she bends, grasps the suit's middle in each hand, and heaves. *Lordy.* Worse than panty hose.

Using every muscle in her body, she stretches the spandex over her withered thighs. *OK, again.*

Elbows out, she strains, and it slips up over the slight bulge of her pot. *It never withers.* And out of breath, she rests.

Will you look at that! Her legs extend, so smooth, so slender, and all swirly color. *Positively nubile.*

Energized, she slips arms in its arms, tugging and wiggling till the suit covers her whole body. Exhausting, but never mind, the effort counts as a workout. Well worth the flutter below her breastbone. She wishes she had a pill. How long has it been?

Quick, she zips her breasts in flat, only a minor hitch over the zipper's missing tooth. Her hands glide down smooth sides. "Eat your heart out, Coco Chanel," she says.

Wilbur shakes the curtain. "Hurry up."

Red-topped hunting socks on, she stomps into the boots' calf-high leather. *With hooks.* None of those pesky holes to thread, she locks the laces tight, ending with a bow.

Ready for combat, she sashays from the booth, nothing binding in inconvenient places. Not that her johnny did, but she found the airiness unsettling.

Wilbur skips down the aisle of clothes. "Take a gander at this," he says. He shakes blue plastic squares above his head. He stops. "Wow, you're dazzling."

"Knee pads," she says and reaches high. The blue matches Hank's cape. She kisses Wilbur's cheek. "You're the best." *Crawling will be a breeze.*

He pays up, adding the hat, a bowl and glass, and out the door, like a puppy with a bone, Wilbur follows Maggie. He carries the bag, her coat over one arm, wingtips under the other. "Now that's successful shopping."

"Your coat," he waves the mink, the phone cord snaking from its sleeve.

"Who cares?" Spandex—it's a whole new luxury, though walking in kneepads takes getting used to.

"You'll get cold; put on your coat."

"And hide this?" She spreads her arms and clomps in a circle. "Never." There'd be no hiding the swirls of hazard-yellow, electric pink, and day-glow green slicked to her body.

"Mesmerizing," he says. "A feast for the eye."

Gone are the days of mother-in-law-beige and keeping her mouth shut. She's free to do as she pleases, giddily free.

CHAPTER 19

HANK

Thursday

Outside, tires screech. From bed, Hank reads his number-clock, eight-zero-zero. A car stops by the front walk.

Up out of bed, he rushes to the window. "Jeremy."

Still dressed from last night except for shoes, Hank heads for the bedroom door. His cape slips. He feels for his mask. Odd, it's on the bedside table. He reties his cape. No time to adjust the mask; it hangs around his neck. He beetles downstairs.

In the front room, Uncle R drags himself off the sofa. He slept in his clothes, too. "I'm leaving," he says, and into the kitchen, "Meet you in town, Clair. No time to waste." And without a sound, he's gone out the back.

"Hank," Ma calls. "Breakfast."

He zooms out the front door, cape flying. His yellow shirt blazes green lightning. Jeremy scoops him off the walk and carries him in.

"You came!" Hank wraps his arms around Jeremy's neck, mask squashed against his chest, and they enter the kitchen.

"It's time to find Nana." Jeremy looks behind the kitchen door. "Where's Roger?" He plops Hank on a stool at the counter next to Ben and Sasha eating the last of their cereal.

"In town." Ma spills Cheerios into a bowl for Hank. "He's searching." She rubs puffy eyes. "I've got to go. Jeremy, please take Hank to school. Then join us."

"Nooo," Hank wails. "I'll search, too."

Ma grabs her coat from a hook by the back door. "We'll start at the hospital, call when you get there." Running out, she waves her clam.

Jeremy holds the door. "What about Sash and Ben?"

"Bus picks them up, they're on their own." She revs the engine and backs out the drive.

"Eat up." Jeremy pours milk on Hank's Cheerios, another bowl for himself. He settles on a stool and digs in.

A horn sounds from the street. Ben and Sasha, their last bites of breakfast unfinished, run for their backpacks in the hall. The front door slams.

"Uncle R must have a bellyache." Hank picks a Cheerio off the counter and puts it on his tongue. "No breakfast, and he didn't wait. Why?"

Jeremy takes a breath. "Can you keep a secret?"

"Sure." Torture couldn't make Amazing Man tell. He resets his mask over his eyes.

Jeremy scooches close. "He's scared."

"Of what?"

"Himself, I guess." Jeremy drops his spoon in the bowl. "He didn't call, your ma did. I love your ma, always worrying about someone else. I had to come."

"Nana says you're through hanging around."

"That's why I went on 'vacation.'"

Kind of like Dad. "But you're best friends; I don't get it."

"Think of it this way." Jeremy stirs his cereal like it's ice cream. "You have a friend, the best, and you're both starving." He slides the bowl half way toward Hank.

"Your friend has ice cream. It melts in a bowl on the table between you, and he won't share. Worse yet, he won't eat it himself.

"I'd eat it." Hank dips out a spoonful of Jeremy's Cheerios and downs it.

"Me, too, so I went to Vermont. There's lots of ice cream there."

"Ma has Chunky Monkey in the freezer."

"Not my favorite flavor." He takes back his bowl. "Eat up now."

Hank stirs a swirl of "Os" in the milk. "Can you guess where Nana's hiding?"

"Your ma thinks she's lost on Beacon Hill."

"That's Boston, right? She should have told me."

Jeremy taps Hank's spoon. "Eat."

"Ma's looking wrong. In Boston, Nana visits Mrs. Mallard."

"Your ma says, 'Nana knows not to go in a park at night.'"

"It's not night, so we start there or at the swan boats, she loves them."

"What's this "we"?" says Jeremy.

"You and me, we'll find her."

"You're going to school."

"Please, Jeremy, we have to. Besides I know *all* her favorite places; she takes me lots. Pleeeease!"

"I'll stash my stuff, then we'll talk." Starting for the stairs he says, "That duck better not be in the toilet."

Headed for school in Jeremy's car, Hank says, "You promised. You promised we'd talk."

"And we did, but you belong in school."

"What's the good of school?" Hank leans over the driver's seat, his mouth close to Jeremy's ear. "I can't think there, not with Nana gone."

"Sit back and use the seatbelt."

Hank flops against the seat and clicks the belt. "Ma says the police won't..." He can't stop his tears. "Everyone has to look, it's the only way."

"Oh, Hank, don't cry." Jeremy reaches behind him and puts a hand on Hank's knee. "I'll make you a deal. We'll search the park. If we don't find her by eleven, you're back in school for lunch."

"Deal!" Hank wipes a sleeve across his eyes.

In the city, stretching the seatbelt, Hank taps Jeremy's shoulder. "Nana said she'd take me there," he says pointing out the passenger side window. His cape, in folds over his arm, hangs like a bat wing.

"The Taj?"

"She calls it Ritz. A place full of crackers, I guess."

"Ah, a parking space." After turning left, Jeremy squeezes the car in a space beside the park. "Your ma better not see us; she'd kill me. Then you."

Hank hops from the back seat onto the sidewalk. "Yeah, no booster seat." He fits the mask over his eyes, his cape flowing from his jacket shoulders. "Look, the swan boats. Nana's special treat." He latches onto Jeremy's hand and hauls him through oncoming walkers. No one else cuts off toward the dock, only them, down the boards to the little house. "Damn, it's empty." Hank stamps his foot. His mask slips. He straightens it and turns in a slow circle, eyeing around the park.

They walk and walk, checking behind trees and statues, around the pond, and under the blue bridge. By the time they get to Mrs. Mallard, Hank is near tears again. "We should have found her by now."

"I hate to say it, but we have to go back. It's way after eleven and that was the deal."

Noooo," Hank wails. Pushing people aside, he takes off at a dead run.

Sprinting after, Jeremy grabs for his hand. "Wait."

"No, no," Hank shouts and dodges. "Nana," he screams. "Where are you?"

"Hey you." Two men in blue rush them from the bridge. "Hold it right there."

One cop catches Hank. "You're OK now, son."

Hank struggles. "Stop. We can't lose her."

"Lose who?"

"Nana—she's here. I know she is. I won't leave. Please, don't let him take me." Frantic, he looks at Jeremy.

The other cop has Jeremy's arm cranked behind his back.

"You've got to help find her."

Jeremy stands on tiptoes, his mouth open. "You've got it wrong," he squeaks.

"And how's that?"

"I'm his friend...his sitter."

"Yeah, sure." Jeremy's cop looks at Hank's cop. "He likes 'em young, huh?"

"Ask his mother, she…" Jeremy points through the gate to the hill of houses. "She'll tell you."

"No, not Ma." Hank tries to pull away. "You said she'd kill you."

Jeremy groans. "Because," he says very slowly to the cop, their faces almost touching, "Hank's supposed to be in school. We're searching for his grandmother, Margaret Colton."

"A likely story."

CHAPTER 20

MAGGIE

Still Thursday

Her feet shod for combat, Maggie prances through the parking lot, Wilbur beside her, holding her coat, shoes, and hat in the plastic bag. "Now you're set, no matter where you live," he says.

"Aren't I living with you?" She peers in his eyes for an answer, but a black minivan at the intake truck stops her.

Cold crawls through her veins. Her boots halt mid-prance, an end to the elation of spandex. Hearses and hockey sticks flash in Maggie's head. "My coat, I'll take it."

Shivering, she snatches the mink, and slips her arms into the furry sleeves. She overlaps the front, winding the cord around her middle, crimping the silk.

Wilbur takes her hand. "What's the matter?" he says.

She stands rooted to the asphalt. "I'm sorting."

"Sorting what?"

She scuffs a heavy boot. The toe hits a beer can, clattering it under the closest car. "Houses," she says, "and hearses and hockey sticks. Do they make sense to you?"

"No."

"Me neither." Anger rattles her. It's not the misremembering; it's the items themselves.

The rear door of the black minivan rises, and a red-eyed woman with pouchy cheeks climbs from the driver's seat. She brushes a patch of dust from her blue coat and straightens dark hair.

At the rear of the van, her back straining, the woman unwedges a green garbage bag from under the roof.

"What a haul," Wilbur whispers to Maggie.

"You must be moving," says the intake man. He reaches from high on his truck, lifts her armload, and tosses it into the depths.

The woman gives a polite smile. As she turns for another trip to the van, she faces in Maggie's direction.

Maggie gapes. She digs her fingers into Wilbur's arm. "My God," she says. "Miss goody-two-shoes." *Did she really think I wouldn't catch her?*

"Ouch." Wilbur yanks from her grip. "What are you saying?"

"Shush." She covers his mouth. Her lips to his ear she hisses, "That's... that's...dark...dark-haired... oh shit, what is her name?"

The woman's gaze passes over Wilbur, over Maggie and down to the asphalt, as if they didn't exist. In her other life, Maggie had done the same when confronted with members of the city's down-and-out, a kind of embarrassment of possessions. A need to disappear herself.

In catching an eye of the homeless, she'd have had to admit a person lived under the dirt; a living, breathing human being behind the blackened eye and broken glasses, the kind of person she couldn't imagine and certainly never expected to be.

Oh right, dark-haired Clair. Clair wouldn't expect it either, so even if she truly looked, Maggie knew she wouldn't see her mother beneath bruises and spandex, sashaying through Goodwill's parking lot. Never mind combat boots and kneepads.

In a blind state, the woman returns to her stuffed van, shoving a stack of framed pictures leaning on their sides.

"Those...those are my pictures." Maggie claws at Wilber's arm, points with the other hand at a piece of picture frame showing gold from under a blanket. "It's an original, for God's sake, my Hudson River."

Those antiques in Goodwill—clarity—a hammer blow. "My stuff, all of it." *Damn her.* Maggie lunges for the van.

Dropping the bag, Wilbur hops in her path. She pushes him. She darts left. His arms out, he blocks her, then folds his arms around her. "What are you doing?" He stands firm. "Think."

Looking over his shoulder, she's stiff in his arms. "It's mine, I'm sure."

"What are you going to do, attack her and take it?"

Maggie struggles.

"And do what with it? Hijack the van and live in it? Sleep on your bags of stuff?"

Maggie is near tears. "She can't give it away, it's not right."

"You have a choice, your possessions or your freedom."

She unstiffens. Without home, there's no place to put it. But Clair's stealing her past faster than Maggie can lose it on her own.

"So, what do you want?" He holds Maggie's upper arms.

"I know what I don't want. I don't want to sleep on Clair's futon, and I don't want some urine-soaked Home."

"Then walk away."

The woman carries a box brimming with Calphalon pans and mason jars. Empty jars. She's thrown away the pickled eggs and beets Maggie preserved, the candied ginger, her jars of ranch dressing doctored with balsamic vinegar and sesame oil.

"Nice," the intake man says, holding a leafy landscape in a black frame. "I'd keep this."

"Downsizing, what can I say?" The woman seems to work at hearty cheer. "Out with the old, in with the new," she says, her back carefully positioned toward Maggie.

"Can't be easy."

"It's not," she says, the false cheer gone. "For my mother, especially."

"Into The Home?" The man laughs and leans against the wall of the truck. "My mom went." He gouges between his front teeth with his littlest fingernail. "She loves it, hanging out in her jammies, and all the Ensure she can drink."

"Anywhere away from him would be heaven," says Wilbur.

The woman drops a black plastic bag. It breaks at her feet, and a pile of woven rainbow potholders Maggie made in grade school scatters the blacktop, along with pencils, pens, spiral pads filled with pictures. "My potholders."

"You can't take it with you," Wilbur says.

"So I've heard, but I'm not dead yet."

Her past litters the pavement. She'd like to touch those triggering things for the last time, replay the lost events.

One touch, and her adventure with Wilbur would come to an end. She would become the living-dead. *Or is it the dead-living?*

She'd best leave the past to some other shopper's future. One last look and through the driver's open door she sees, on the passenger seat, a gray plastic carrier with the metal grate open.

"Clair!" Maggie screams. She launches herself at the woman's back, dragging Wilbur in the process. "What have you done with Clyde?"

The woman retreats, flattening against the van. "I think you're…"

"You've no right," Maggie shrills. "Get him back or I'll…"

"Please." The woman shrinks from Maggie's strangling fingers. "Please stop." Her back against the car, hands in high surrender, she sidles away. "I'm Sarah; I… I promise."

Most of the way back to Wilbur's, Maggie sheds tears of embarrassment. She'd been shown up close the stuff in the van, all very much like hers, but not. The woman had cried, too.

"Thank God that's over," says Wilbur. They cross the street and enter the alley.

But free of Clair means no more Hank, her once and always hero.

Crawling back into Wilbur's hidey-hole, Maggie misses her sneak-around buddy. Even kneepads don't ease the pain.

For Hank, could she give up her freedom?

Who will intercede for him? Without Maggie, who will take him seriously? Does Clair even see him, the him inside of his head? The place where his friends live.

Though the youngest, he's more adult than Hockey-Boy, more empathic than Trumpet-Girl, and less prone to nightmares after watching *Night in the Museum,* his all-time favorite. Yet Clair ordered him to bed when she found him watching through the banister. It wasn't fair. What will happen to Hank?

After a late morning nap, Maggie swims in a sea of memory, comfy in Wilbur's bed, except that she hates how her pillow falls over the open end.

"Up and at 'em," says Wilbur as he pushes a mattress through the entrance. He gives a Vanna White swing of his arm at a slab of Styrofoam leaning against the wall. "You'll need this," he says. "Cement sweats. I thought I'd peed my first bed." He hurries both pieces deep into the tunnel.

"For me?" she asks. "From Goodwill?"

"Not exactly." *Which question did he answer?*

In the dimmer reaches beyond the beanbag chair, she helps him stack the bed. "Head at the brick, can't have my pillow escape."

"You'll need another light," he says and retrieves a bag from the entrance. "And sheets." He flaps open a field of overlapping orange and black.

"Sunflowers!" she crows and fits the fitted corners over the mattress.

"That's all they had." Wilbur flings out the top sheet. "Noisy colors, I'd never sleep."

"This is mine?" She tucks in the sheet with a hospital corner. *I'll put up a curtain here, hooks there, my johnny...* "Mine forever?"

"Quite a question for a first date." He plumps her pillow.

"Is this a date?"

"Maybe," he says. "I can't think on an empty stomach."

One block, two blocks, street after street, she loses count, and at his favorite restaurant, they slip into the alley. *A dumpster, I should have known.*

"You lift the lid," he says. "I'll dive." Hanging over the metal edge, he assures her he knows the look of bags with the freshest pie, the warmth of the oven, not the heat of festering.

Feet waving, from the depths he says, "What's your favorite? His question echoes in the bin.

He lifts out a cleanish cardboard, and belly on the edge, slides to the ground. "Disappointing." He lays a slice of pepperoni and pineapple on the cardboard. "Let's eat at the library."

"They let you?"

"In the yard." He leads her down the widest street to a little brick library, the yard out front with benches and bushes and mothers shepherding toddlers.

"Pineapple's not for me," he says. "You want mine?"

Maggie wrinkles her nose. He flicks the offending morsels to birds collecting at their feet. Two bites each and the slice is gone.

Maggie lounges on the bench. She's been here before, a play yard then, little Clair climbing the block structure. Rog in a stroller. *The South End.*

How she loved living in the South End, the brick houses, the endless renovations with Victorian details she freed from generations of paint. She reclaimed arched doorframes, crown moldings, ornate ceiling medallions. Uncountable times a day, she ascended and descended five floors on a sweeping staircase.

I'm still hungry," says Wilbur. "Let's go."

They ogle rows of joined houses as they walk. Was it yesterday she picked at that flowered medallion, freeing veined-leaves hidden under the paint? "I love the medallions."

Wilbur nods. "Curry House has two. AND FOOD." He licks his lips. "A real dinner, that's what we'll have."

"Curry House? Spicy doesn't like me." Maggie rubs her belly. "Not anymore."

"No curry, it's one of those Godly places." He pulls her around a corner and stops. "Keep your head down. The short guy, he'll talk your ear off. Buzz-cut's better, but he'll get in your face and ask you to read."

CHAPTER 21

HANK

Still Thursday

The cops ruined everything. All that time wasted getting to Ma, when Nana had to be right near.

At school, Hank sits cross-legged in a circle with his class, Ms. Hegger yammering about numbers. He has more important things on his mind, like how to get back to the park. He'd been so close, and no matter what he said, no one listened.

Even Jeremy. If only he'd yelled at the police instead of telling Hank to be quiet.

And they hurt him. That cop marched Jeremy the whole way to Ma. Mrs. G only pinched Hank's ear when she'd marched him to the sidewalk, and that was bad.

Jeremy offered the phone, but his phone wasn't real enough. The cop said, "Identification in person."

Jeremy drove one-handed to school, and no amount of pleading could make him take Hank back to the park.

He'd lost his best chance. Now, he's on his own, his plan solid as Jell-O. Major Amazing Man should be able to fly, once he escapes Ms. Hegger.

The carpool line, that's it. Ms. Hegger's eye will be on some other troublemaker.

In class, she holds up a big yellow card. "Hank," she says, all warm and soft, different since he came back from the park, not like how she talks to the other kids. It makes him want to cry.

"I know you know this number?" She holds the card, one she'd just drawn, low and easy to see, a number much bigger than usual.

No need to think, he just says, "Twenty-four." Yes, he knows it from TV, thanks to Uncle R and his reruns.

Hank's attention sneaks out the window to the growing carpool line. If he's quick, he can slip out when kids mob the double doors. With all the hoop-la, no one will see he's gone, not till Ma heads the line; and she's not there. Not yet.

But wow, that first car— racy red, a two-seater. He cranes taller for a better look through the window. Cool. A man climbs out and sits on the front fender. "Holy Cow!" Dad!

He doesn't do pick-up. And what about Ma?

"Hank," Ms. Hegger lays her hands on his shoulders. "Easy now, it's going to be all right."

The bell rings. Hank, out from under her hands, makes a dash. "My Dad's here, gotta go." On his way, he pops his backpack off its hook, and ahead of everyone, runs across the waiting area. "Dad," he shouts. "Dad. Where's Ma?" Nana missing is scary enough. "Where is she?"

"What kind of greeting is this?"

"What's happened?" Hank pushes his backpack at Dad.

"Thought I'd show you the new car; give you a ride home. We'll meet Ma later."

Cripe. Hank could've escaped.

"Get in."

"I'm not s'pposed to ride shotgun."

"No back seat, you'll have to." Dad holds the door. He taps Hank on the rump. "In you go."

From the other side of the car, he shouts to Hank's teacher, "Bye, Mrs. Hatfield, I've got Hank."

"That's Ms. Heg—"

The engine roars, tires chirp, and he's off the mark. "How about this?" he says and pats the dashboard.

Hank, his backpack between his feet, grips the seatbelt at his chest. If he doesn't, the thing creeps up till he chokes.

"Corners like a dream, right?" says Dad.

Hank slides against the door. With a grab at Hank's collar, Dad rights him. The other hand cranks the wheel, same at every turn.

At home, he screeches to a stop, blocking the driveway. "She's a beauty." He turns off the engine. "A surprise for your Ma."

Sure surprised Hank.

"A peace offering." Dad pulls a lever. "Want to see the engine?"

Hank hears the gas door pop.

"Oops." Dad searches under the dash, slides his hand down the driver's well. "Ah, here."

Out of the car, he lifts the hood and pokes around. "Check out this carburetor," he says, as if he knows what it does. "Yes sir." He claps Hank on the back. "Six speed, V8."
"That's a drink, isn't it?" It's the only V8 Dad knows. Ben says the V is for Vodka.

"Eight hundred horses all here under the hood, bluetooth, and navigation." He twirls the key with its Corvette logo. Ben has one like it, a logo, not the car.

"In the house, come on." At the front door, Dad presses the latch. "She locks the door now?" He pulls out a ring of keys. The first one doesn't slide in. "Huh." He flips through five and chooses another. "Fuck." One more. "So, that's how it is."

Here comes Ma parking by the sidewalk, the van big and black. Ben's right, it does look like a hearse.

Dad turns from the door. "What the hell, Clair?" He shakes his keys at her. "You're changing everything, the living room, the dining room, a new bathroom! Now the locks?

"Sorry," she says, all sing-songy. "I didn't realize you'd be home." She steps flagstone to flagstone up the walk. "And you picked up Hank, how nice."

Hank's never seen this super sweet side. Sweet as I-Hop's double dip French toast with bananas, peanut butterscotch sauce, whip cream, and chocolate bits. It turns his stomach.

"You're locking me out," Dad says, "when I brought you a peace offering?" He points at the Corvette.

"We'll discuss this another time." She takes out her keys. "Hank needs a snack." Hank couldn't stomach a bite.

Dad blocks the door. "Come on, Clair. You believe in second chances, don't you?"

"I do, but what would this be? The fifth, the seventh?"

"You and your locks, you started this," he says. "Now I'm going to finish it." He clamps an arm on Hank's shoulder. "I want custody."

Inside the house Zip goes ballistic, barking and snarling from his perch on the back of the sofa.

Sure, Zip doesn't like Dad, but this... Oh, of course, here comes Fluffy rubbing against Dad's leg. He sidesteps, white hairs on his pants.

"You're unfit." Dad brushes at the cat hair. "You can't keep track of one old lady, never mind three kids." He slaps his hands together. "And child support. You have two jobs. I want child support."

"So that's what this is: money! Try selling the car."

"I would if I owned it."

Red lights flash, gears grind, and the school bus stops behind Ma's car. The doors fold open.

"Ben," Dad calls. He waves both arms, a real train stopper.

Kids pile out, Ben first down the walk. Dad spreads his arms. Ben brushes by and puts his key in the lock.

"What, no hug for your old man? And I brought you a car."

Ben opens the door. "Maybe tomorrow, 'old man,' if you're still around." He slams the door.

"Daddy, Daddy." Sasha hugs him.

Sure, Ma always says he's the only dad they have, so be nice. But he turned Sasha's tuba into a lamp. How can she be nice?

Crushing her to his chest, Dad mouths over her head, "Custody."

"What about Nana?" Hank shouts. "Have you forgotten?" He runs for the street. Dad catches his arm, swings him off his feet and into a three-way hug with Sasha. "You'll live with me, give your ma more time to look for Nana."

"Sure thing," says Ma, giving Dad the hairiest eyeball ever. "Good idea. *You* take them. No time like the present. Have the van, too, I won't need it; and be sure Ben packs all his hockey gear. He has practice Tuesdays, Thursdays, Fridays, and a game Saturday afternoon. Hank has a check-up with the pediatrician on Wednesday; Sasha goes to trumpet lessons on Thursdays. I'll send you further schedules." She unlocks the door. "Better let the school know. You'll have to drive them to and from until you find a bus route."

"What?" Dad drops Hank and Sasha on the walk. "Well— wait a minute. I—"

"No!" Hank stumbles over to Ma. He wraps his arms tight around her waist, the side of his face squashed against her.

She bends to his ear, her hairy-eye still on Dad. "Not to worry," she whispers. "It won't happen. Not ever."

Sasha stares at Ma, her mouth open. Dad takes two steps away and twists toward the van, then back toward Ma. He checks his watch. "I have to... When I..." He bolts for his car. "I'll catch you later."

"I doubt that," says Ma as the car zooms off.

"You wouldn't let him," Sasha says. "Would you?"

"Never!" Ma pulls her in beside Hank. "He may be your father, and you can visit whenever you want, but I'm your mother, and you're living with me."

"All we need now," Hank says as he squeezes Ma, "is Nana."

CHAPTER 22

MAGGIE

Thursday Dinner to Friday Morning

At Curry House, Maggie passes the set of stone stairs, curly metal railings on both sides, and starts down a narrow set to an arched doorway below.

"Upstairs," Wilbur says. "We're guests of honor. We eat in the dining room."

Up the steep granite, her palms press spandex-covered knees. She counts each step. Her big boots echo down the block. Out of breath by the eighth, she rests before braving the next three. At the top, she twists the knob on the ornate door.

Inside, the place has been gutted, front windows to the rear alley. Paint peels on what's left of two medallions. Rough patches splotch the walls, and the floor shows where walls once stood. Five long tables fill the space, eight folding chairs on each side.

"Kitchen's in the basement," says Wilbur, as three men appear from the stairway at the far end. At the furthest table, the men lift lids off steaming metal trays.

Maggie and Wilbur join the grungy line of diners shuffling toward the hot meal. A man behind each tray serves with a large spoon. Mac-and-cheese wafts through the room, its warm comfort spiked with the scent of overcooked greens, like spinach but worse.

Their plates full, they find seats at a middle table. Maggie pushes the greens to the edge of her plate; she won't have them touching the orange elbows. Despite Wilbur's warning, she can't resist a quick peek around.

A heavy-set woman lowers herself on Maggie's left, the folding chair groaning as she reaches for the bread in the center of the table. Two black-suited men wander among the tables. Hand on a back there, on a shoulder here, they lean over whispering in ear after ear. If one approaches, Maggie hopes it's Buzz-cut; his face is kinder, sadder, not so overbearing.

Not so the other one, his arm stiff and prodding. She can't hear the words he pushes at a bent-backed diner, but the balding man flinches, attention glued to his plate. Who is this diner? She knows him, or does she? How is it she recognizes people she doesn't know, and can't remember the people she should?

Maggie digs into the macaroni, the cheese thick and gooey, real cheese. Why has she suddenly lost her appetite?

She pokes the army-green greens curling beside the macaroni. "What's that?" she asks Wilbur.

"Kale," he says. "Poor man's spinach."

A leaf droops on her fork. She nibbles. "It's horr...."

"Fssst." The woman on her left nudges Maggie.

"What?"

A hand rests gently on Maggie's back. She's afraid to lift her eyes in case it's the wrong guy.

"You're new here," he says.

"Mmmm." She nods at her plate. He has a nice voice, something about it, comforting.

"Would you do us the honor of reading a psalm?"

She shakes her head, no. Now the meal calls her.

His hand stays at the base of her neck. "It would be a kindness."

What she's eaten is already beyond any kindness she can repay, and he isn't asking her to convert. As far as the Bible goes, she rather enjoys the stories.

He presses the open book into her hands, the worn leather soft, the pages onionskin thin, the print small.

The letters flow together. She coughs. The words look familiar, but when her tongue sounds them, she realizes no real words emerge. They tease and tantalize. She tries again. Squinting, she adjusts her crooked glasses.

Wilbur takes the book. "It's hard with a black eye," he says. He shoves his chair back into the minister, "Excuuuuse me," and blocks him from Maggie. "My friend doesn't speak English."

"We have the Bible in Spanish." He hustles for the stairs to the kitchen.

"Don't bother," Wilbur shouts after him. "She's Latvian."

At the stairs, Buzz-cut collides with a man coming up. Long dark hair held in a low ponytail. He hugs Buzz-cut. Buzz glances around as if caught at mischief.

"What are you doing here?" he says, hurrying the guy down and out of sight.

Undaunted by murmurs through the group, Wilbur reads the 23rd Psalm in a monotone and closes the book. Maggie scrapes up the last cheese with her spoon.

"Why not lick it?" he says, and she does. "Jesus, that was a joke."

"Waste not, want not."

"I suppose you'll want rice pudding, too." Wilbur pushes his plate to the middle of the table.

"Not really." She wipes her mouth with a paper napkin.

"Let's go before we're trapped."

At the door, he says, "Ooo, wait a minute." He runs back to the serving table, returning with his hands behind his back.

Out on the stoop, Wilbur sits on the top step. He pats the stone beside him. "Guess what I found?" He sounds like Hank.

Maggie sits. "A rubber chicken?" She leans back, trying to see behind him. "A live frog?"

"Nooo, silly," he says and whips out a chocolate cupcake with sprinkles on top.

Her eyes swim, and there is Dear Dead Dan in the kitchen, clear as if he sits on the stoop.

₧₧

When Dan perched on a stool, he looked like Bob Cratchit. Instead of accounting on a ledger, he worked laboriously inserting upright spikes of chocolate into the iced top of a cupcake, the cake shaped like a hedgehog. "*I* made it!" he said with a grin.

"Pretty pleased with yourself, aren't you?" He'd hit on the perfect birthday present. She ran her arms around him from the back and kissed his neck while her fingers crawled toward his belt.

"At this rate, I'll..."

And every year thereafter he celebrated his success with a tiny ceramic replica.

⊱⊰

"Maggie, I'm sorry," says Wilbur. "I thought you liked chocolate."

"I do," she croaks. She clears her throat. "Let's eat."

He peels the paper off one half and holds it up. "You take the first bite," he says, an endearing tilt to his head.

Wilbur pops the second half of the cupcake into his mouth. Through crumbs he asks, "Where should we go now?" Maggie sits beside him, legs out, knees locked. Twisting her boots right then left, she admires the multi colored swirls of spandex flowing around her thighs and shins.

A desperate voice floats up from the stairwell below, "...any little thing sets me off."

"You're scared," says a deeper voice.

"I took it out on her."

"And me as well; it's what you do."

"I'm sorry." The voice cracks and fades.

A sigh rises from the well. "I thought losing her slowly couldn't be worse. This is beyond worse. And... something else."

Silence falls. Maggie wonders if they've gone inside.

"...a confession."

"Poor guy," Wilbur whispers. "Thank God, I'm too old for a girlfriend."

Maggie punches his arm. "No one's too old for love."

"So says you."

The deep voice rises, suddenly loud. "Get rid of it? No. It's not just hers. And if she doesn't want it, *I do*."

"If she keeps it, marriage is...."

"Jesus," the deep voice says, "is this the fifties?"

"Too much for me," says Wilbur. He takes Maggie's hand. "Come on, let's window-shop."

She tiptoes, as much as tiptoeing is possible in combat boots, down the stairs and off to Tremont, slipping into a stream of afternoon gawkers.

೮೦ᏨᏀ

Wilbur's nose always drips, Maggie's too, but that evening his turns to a rattling cough he stifles in his pillow. Maggie presses her hand to his forehead. "You need soup, lots of hot soup." She retrieves his panda PJs. "Supper in bed for you."

She lines up four cans on the counter, chicken, chicken noodle, chicken and rice, beef barley. Latching the can opener onto the rim of the chicken noodle, she twists the handle. The blade rolls a halting grind around half the can. She flexes stiff knuckles. *I'll never get through four.* Taking a break, she changes into her johnny.

Back at the counter she pries at the lid with a knife, slips her fingers under, thumb on top, and bends it enough to dump the soup. Same for the second, though not even halfway around with the opener. For the third can, the opening is smaller still. She barely gets her fingers under the lid, and as she pries, the can tilts. Her fingers slip.

"Aaaah!" The lid slices the tips of three fingers, and soup splashes the shelf. *Damn-it.*

At first, it's chicken soup wetting her fingers, then blood wells. It runs down her hand. She wraps her fingers in the johnny's hem, pressing them into a fist. With the other hand, she pours the remains of the soup into the pan and turns on the heat. Three cans will have to do.

Maggie knows she should keep applying pressure. It always takes longer to clot than you'd think. Patience a virtue in short supply, she opens her fist and lifts the blood-soaked cloth.

"Please," says Wilbur. "No blood in the soup."

"You can use the protein," she says, and sure enough the blood wells again. Using a clean section of johnny, she rewraps her fingers, no blood near the soup. She pours and passes the bowl to Wilbur. "Drink it all or I'll have to feed you."

"You'll drown me."

"Drown the cough," she corrects. "Liquid in, liquid out."

In the meantime, on the Kaopectate shelf, she finds Band-Aids. Just four left. What a mess, blood on the box and the shelf. The paper wrapping slips as she tries to tear it open, and once open there's blood on the sticky part. It won't stick to her finger.

She rewraps in the johnny. Waits longer. And longer still. Unwrapping, she examines the cuts. The tips of her fingers gape in dry little smiles. She opens the Band-Aids using a scissors this time. The first one goes on fine. The second covers ooze, and she sticks it quick. The third finger flows freely. She dries it with the johnny, sticks on the covering, and again puts pressure on all three.

With the scissors handy, she may as well cut the ID band off her wrist. Cutting with her left hand isn't easy. She makes a hash of it and throws it in the trash with the bloody box and wrappers.

After more waiting, she changes back into the spandex. She'll have to wash the johnny later. After wadding up the bloody mess by her bed, she drags the beanbag chair to Wilbur's bedside. Reading is restorative.

All those books at home in her library, going to waste with no one to hold them. Such a shame. They took her to other worlds, no cramped airline seats, no expensive tickets. No search for the next reasonable bathroom.

She'd open a book and smell the paper, the scent of home and far-away places all in one whiff, the heavy stock fine and smooth between her fingers as she turned the pages. She reveled in the slow flicker of firelight, her only living, breathing companion except Clyde.

She curls in the beanbag and opens Billy Collins in her lap. The humor bubbles through them as she turns each page with care. Blood on the book would be a sacrilege.

"I used to write," she admits. "Childish ditties, my teacher called them."

"Too bad," Wilbur says. "You might have been the Paul Klee of poetry."

She snorts. "I pulled a Sylvia Plath."

Wilbur looks horrified. "You didn't kill yourself?"

"Am I dead?" She looks over the top of the book. "No, I killed my drivel."

Maggie's darlings had filled the night like a dripping spigot, and finally went dry from lack of encouragement.

"You didn't save any?"

"In my desk drawer. I read it over lots—a reminder of old aspirations."

"Let's hear it," Wilbur says. "I won't laugh."

She rubs her palms together, and much to her surprise the poem hops onto her tongue. "Really?" she says.

"Don't be shy. Do it."

"It *is* drivel. "I can't."

"What's the worst that can happen?" He touches her knee.

She's six, a first-grader called on to read. The worst, then, was not knowing how. The worst now is losing the words. But here they are, waiting. *So, what the hell.*

"American Bunnies

Snow Bunny: garish coloration; inhabits low slopes; lacks coordination
Dust Bunny: prolific; housebound; hard to exterminate
Road Bunny: flat pelt on the beltway
Bilge Bunny: found below decks; prone to gastronomic distress
Bunny Hop: spasmodic illness transmitted to humans

Playboy Bunny: nearly hairless; found in folds; known
for enlarged mammaries
Easter Bunny: melts when hot; resurrects yearly."

Wilbur laughs. "I know, I said I wouldn't..."

She rather likes his laugh, the warmth. The way it bubbles up
from his core. Kind. Honest.

"It's not Shakespeare, but I like it," he says. "It makes
me happy."

She grins and stretches her swirly legs. *Success of the highest order.*
Not something she ever expected to attain, a completion of who
she is, separate from children, from her husband, something
living in her the way she lives in her own home, a small happiness
yet bigger than a house, waiting all this time for her to find the
perfect listener.

She leans to the bed and kisses his smooth, baby-bald pate.
Only a dish of dark would make for a better evening.

Later, Maggie jolts awake. *Clair's house! Good grief.* For sure, no
amount of chocolate could induce her to go there.

"Wilbur, it's time," she says and hikes onto her knees. She
stands on her mattress. *That lawyer.*

Out of the dark, Wilbur says, "Go back to bed, it's three in
the morning."

Moths crawl in her chest. Tasting their dust, she coughs. This
is her butterflies' flipside; she sees the razor edge sharp at her
feet, the plunge a step away. "We have to go. Now."

CHAPTER 23

CLAIR

Thursday to Friday

In bed, Clair stares at the dark ceiling. "I don't pray," she says. "So, what am I doing?" The plaster hovers above her, weighty plaster she works to see through, wanting something to believe in, a being to sustain her as she wrangles the shifting winds of this new reality.

Frustration and fear had her screaming at the police, who were only trying to help, or so they assured her, when they finally let Jeremy go.

At least Jeremy held her hand after he dropped Hank at school, or was she holding his? He needed comfort after the officers' attention, and Roger's lack of it. Roger insisted they'd be more effective if they spread out.

"Tell me, God, how do I ask?" This need, this seeking, a cure for her unreal reality. "Do I beg? Plead? And why would You listen, what with me coming so late to the party?"

All she wants is the way things were. Hank, his innocent self, unscathed. Mum home, the way she was.

No, that's too much to ask. Not the real Mum, maybe, but Clair will take anything, even the times that drove her the craziest. Yes, she'd welcome them.

How had she let such silly incidents gnaw at her bones?

If only her mother returns, Clair won't mind the constant, "What time is it?" Every five minutes, every three, that's fine.

Clair should have laughed at the daily packages ordered online. Ignored Mum's assurance, "See, anything I want in the catalogue, just call. It's magic."

But Clair groused, returning a dozen pairs of leather gloves in a rainbow of colors, and the four bright pink puffy jackets small enough for Hank. Easy enough to shut down the card.

159

All the cards, once she found them. It didn't matter, yet they shredded her patience.

Bring Mum home, and Clair will be the butt of her mother's helpfulness. No biting back. She'll absorb Mum's announcements in restaurants: "Are you a girl or a boy?" said to the waiter with earrings, breasts, and a crew-cut. And on the way home, "Funny how woman's bodies are more beautiful than men, but not so desirable." Mum with a magpie tip to her head, "Why is that?" Clair did laugh that time. So much aggravation, what she wouldn't give to have it again. A hundred times. A thousand times over. Mum safe in the house.

The next morning, Ben and Sasha step over piles of laundry and head for the cereal cupboard. Sasha takes out Cheerios. Ben opens Froot Loops.

"No Loops, this isn't a weekend."

"Friday, right." He sits at the counter. Clair lifts milk from the fridge and sets the plastic gallon in front of their bowls.

Ben shakes the bottle. "It's empty."

Clair slumps, the day already getting away from her. How can the world continue as if nothing's gone wrong?

"Don't worry, Ma," Ben says. I'll get toast." He tosses the bottle in the trash.

"I want white." Sasha rubs her eyes.

Ben scowls and clicks down the toaster. "Wheat is what there is, and we're out of jam, so cool it."

Clair slides the last of the butter across the counter. Toast pops and they slather it as Hank crosses the laundry, pats Zip, and crawls onto a stool. He yawns.

Another shade darker, and the circles under his eyes would look like someone punched him. "Toast only?" he says, and his brother drops another slice in the toaster.

Ben's helpful protection makes Clair want to cry.

The bus honks from the street. Toast dripping butter through their fingers, jackets off hooks, backpacks slung over shoulders, Sasha and Ben run for it.

"Sorry about the milk, Hank," Clair says. "I'll shop after I drop you at school."

ℬℭ

At Star Market, Clair pushes the cart, its bar sticky with some toddler's snack. The shelves, bright-colored streaks, stretch impossibly long. "Excuse me," say faceless people brushing past. They nudge with a basket. An elbow. They reach across her as she stands.

Focus. Come on.

Check the list.

She forgot the list. No, she never made the list. Milk? Cereal?

She bobs left avoiding an oncomer, bobs right, and still in their way, she dances with deadpan strangers.

Yogurt. Peanut butter. Angel hair pasta. White balsamic. Black sesame seeds.

She plucks a leafy something from a stack of misted greens, drops it in the cart, no plastic protection.

Ice cream. Mum will... Fear breaks in a wave and blots out the freezer case.

She *will* be found. She *will* be. She *will*.

Mum and Hank *will* sit together at the kitchen table. They *will* stir their ice cream to soup. They have to.

They're like twins, born seventy-four years apart, even sharing a love for Lapsang. What kid likes Lapsang? Or tea ceremonies? That's Hank, the kid whose best friends are his hands. The hands he talks to like Mum talks to her portraits.

"My god." Mum does talk to the pictures. All the time. Hank giggled about it after his last visit. Clair chalked it up to her mother's worsening state.

Of course, Clair would think that. Clair's not like her mother or Hank. She misses her friends at the tot-lot, how they shared survival tips, from crisping flaccid lettuce to signs of infidelity.

But if talking to non-human friends is delusional, what does that say about Hank? He isn't delusional. So, what does that say about Mum?

Clair had been sure of every sign. What a dolt.

Hank happily plays by himself. He has his hands.

Mum. Would she need the people she'd meet at The Home?

Old friends almost never stopped by. And was she lonely? No.

Not sleeping in the safety of her canopied bed, not having dinner with her portraits, *that* makes her lonely. She'd said as much.

And yesterday, Clair, deaf, dumb, blind Clair, gave Mum's friends away.

"Shit, shit, shit." She flies down the freezer aisle, her cart abandoned in the middle, shoves through the checkout, then wild into the parking lot.

Find them. She'll beat someone bloody if she has to.

CHAPTER 24

MAGGIE

Friday

"Maggie, no lawyer is open at three a.m." Wilbur eases back in bed.

In her own bed, coat pulled to her chin, she stares into the dark.

"Stop huffing," he says. "You can't speed time."

"Mostly, it goes fast." She squirrels around. "Why not now?"

"A watched ceiling won't bring the dawn."

"What makes you so smart?"

"I'm a ceiling specialist. Now go to sleep. That's an order."

ೞ೪

When morning comes, they take turns at cold-water ablutions. Sugar Pops next, hurried by the handful. Wilbur dresses in work clothes, Maggie still in spandex.

"Don't you look dapper!" She spins him around. A hand to his forehead, she says, "Feeling better?"

"I'm fine."

"Still too warm."

"Don't fuss," he says. "When we get there, you have to turn your coat right side out."

"Why? It's too cold."

"You won't make it past the entrance." He looks at her feet. "Want your shoes?"

"Boots are best. This is combat."

"Fine, but turn the coat. And wear the hat." He adjusts the wide brim. "Hide the black eye."

"I'll switch at the office, not before."

They sneak down the alley, and on the sidewalk, he asks, "You know where you're going?"

"Get us to the park." Maggie pushes him on. "I'll know the building."

In the Garden, they walk the perimeter again and again, Maggie eyeing each high-rise they pass. "No."

"Still No?"

"No. I mean yes, still no." Her feet drag.

"What about The Common?" Wilbur says.

Hours more, and with the sun way past high, they're a block from the movie theater. "There!" She points high. "That one, with the biggest windows."

"You've seen it a hundred times, are you sure?"

"Yes, I'm sure."

"Good, then turn your coat." He holds her collar.

"So bossy, you're worse than Clair."

"For your own good." He slips the coat off her shoulders.

"That's what she says."

With her coat right-side out, they enter the lobby. She looks at names listed in the glass case. For a better view, she lifts the floppy brim of her hat. "It's something like Fixawitz, Reznick." She runs a finger down the list: "Belcher, Cuddly..."

"No Maggie, that's Cuddy."

"Gilbert...Karp...Mason—Mason, that sounds right."

He rests a hand on her arm. "You're thinking of Perry?"

"If he's Perry Mason, so much the better." She shakes him off. "At least I'll have a lawyer. Fifth floor, let's go." On automatic, she punches the button.

"Floor four."

"I thought you said five?" says Wilbur.

They step from the elevator onto a high pile carpet leading to a door marked Gilbert. "Yes, this is it."

"So, it's not Mason."

"Of course not. That's TV."

Behind a wide mahogany desk sits a busty young woman, topped with a blast of bleached hair. A plaque at the edge of the desk reads "Dawn Sharp."

Wilbur lifts an eyebrow.

Dawn files her thumbnail. "You got an appointment?"

Wilbur leans to Maggie's ear. "Dawn?" he whispers. "She's not your lawyer, is she?"

CHAPTER 25

HANK

Friday

School's half-day done, and home again, Hank gets ready for court. Ma calls up the stairs. "Hurry up."

He clops down the steps in Trumpet-Girl's sparkly shoes. Ma holds his jacket. "No, no!" she says. "*Your* shoes."

When Ma's at court, that's his best chance to slip out. "I need red shoes."

"No."

In his room, he jams his feet into hiking boots. He draws round eyes above his toes. With these, his cape, and mask, he'll be OK.

Oh right, and the pistol. He fishes deep under his mattress, catches the gun, and tucks it detective-style at the back of his belt. The cape covers it.

"No cape," Ma says when he gets downstairs. "No mask either."

He sits on the bottom step, elbows on his knees. "Then I'm not going."

"For God's sake."

Hank doesn't budge.

"OK, OK. Just go." She hurries him out the door just as a black flash slips between their feet and on toward the kitchen. "Oh, Clyde, thank God!"

Hank runs after him, both stopping at the empty bowl. "He needs food."

"We're late," Ma says. On the fly she splatters kibble in the bowl, half on the floor, and hauls Hank back to the door. At the car she says, "In."

He balks. "His food, Zip's gonna steal it." He braces against the doorframe.

"You're a piece of work." Ma shoves him into his seat and pulls the strap across his chest. The pistol digs at his back. It hurts.

Detectives don't sit in booster seats. Tough it out.

"What's wrong with you?" Ma pushes his chest. "Lean back." The seatbelt clicks.

Wiggling, he shifts the pistol sideways. He thanks his heroes that this gun isn't huge.

"You better be good," Ma says. "No funny business."

"Funny business?" he whispers to his hand.

His fingers open and close against his thumb. *What could she mean?*

"Like pulling a pistol?" he says.

"Right." Ma starts the car, and they're off.

The whole way in to Boston, he memorizes Gulf and Sunoco, tall landmarks and malls. He'll find his way home.

Ma drives into the underground garage. "Mask in the car," she says. "You don't want to lose it. Here, take your bus." The double-decker toy fits neatly in his hand, but he needs both hands. He clamps the bus in his armpit and tosses his mask on the seat.

When Ma puts the parking ticket in her purse, he swipes the mask, stuffs it into his jacket pocket, and hops out onto hard cement.

Hank presses "UP" in the elevator. Outside in the light, he asks, "Ma, what store does Nana shop at?"

"Why?" Ma eyes him. Detective eyes. He's a criminal under the lights.

"Hey, I'm a good guy," he says.

Right, she can't tell. His jacket covers the cape, all but the blue end hanging to the backs of his knees.

He'd like her help. "Ma, would you..."

But Peter Parker never asked his aunt. Bruce Wayne and Batman didn't have a mother between them.

"What is it, Hank?" Ma takes his hand. She hurries him across the street.

"Nothing, Ma."

Major Amazing Man goes it alone.

CHAPTER 26

MAGGIE

Still Friday

"She's not anyone's lawyer. I'm not sure she's even a secretary."

"I'm a temp receptionist. And you are?"

By the window, a small boy, his back to them, crashes a double-decker bus into a chair leg. The place, for all its glitz, smells like an old ashtray.

Wilbur advances. He leans his hands on the desk in front of the nameplate. "Dawn, we'd like to speak…"

"Mr. Gilbert doesn't take walk-ins." She unwraps a stick of gum and folds it in her mouth. "'Sides, he's in court on the Helmsworth…"

Relief floods Maggie. Morty Gilbert helped her buy the house. He'd help her keep it.

"Hey." A little voice attacks Maggie from behind. "You napped my Nana."

Maggie stumbles as fists yank her coattail. Tipping, she swivels and sits on the desk, hands up, one close, protecting her face, the other palm out defending against her masked attacker.

Feet apart, her small assailant snarls, "Give her back, you…"

"Hush up, Hank," says Dawn. "Stop bothering the client."

"Hank?" Maggie lifts her hat.

Hank rocks back on his heels. He shoves up his mask. "Nana?" He stares. "You?"

Oh right, the black eye, the spiked hair.

"In the flesh," she says, and grinning, she holds out her arms.

He rushes in. They hug and hug and hug. "More," she says, and holds tighter.

Dawn sits forward in her chair. "Like, you're his grandmother?" Her continuous yammer floats over Maggie's head as she rocks Hank.

"*What* are you doing here?"

"Waiting, what else?" He shrugs. "Ma's courting, and I'm not allowed."

Dawn snickers.

"Court? Oh, my house! Right." Maggie heads for the elevator. "Wilbur, we've got to go."

"I'll come, too," says Hank.

"No, wait for your Ma." Maggie peels his hand from hers.

"Sit where I told you," says Dawn.

"I want to go with Nana." Looking up at Maggie, Hank folds his hands in prayer. "Please, take me with you."

"If you're like his grandmother…" Dawn says.

"Not 'like' his grandmother, I *am* his grandmother."

"Please, Nana, she smokes on the steps." Hank points out the window.

"You took him on the fire escape?"

"That was the fun part," he says. "Her smoke stinks."

"You can't stay here." Maggie takes his hand. "Let's go, Hank. Come on Wilbur."

"I'm hungry." Hank skips backward in front of her. "Dawn gave me lunch, gum, and seven tic-tacs.

"It's way past lunch; let's have dinner early," says Maggie. "Except we should…" *We should…?*

"Pizza?" Hank opens the door. "Come on."

"I know the perfect place," Wilbur says through a hard cough.

"No dumpster for Hank." Maggie pulls them both to the elevator. "Wilbur makes great soup. Let's go home."

Back in the burrow, Maggie kicks off her boots. Wilbur puts a finger to his lips. "Shhhh," he says. "Remember, you have to whisper; this isn't the Ritz." He coughs with his mouth closed. His cheeks are rosy.

"Nana, this is cool." Hank skips to the edge of the lighted area, tests Maggie's bed with his knee, and returning, runs his double-decker bus across shelf after shelf, through the piles of stones and bright sea glass. Hard confetti showers the floor. He covers his eyes.

"Watch it!" Wilbur's sharp whisper. He scoops the shards off the floor and realigns the piles. Sorrow drags at the corners of his eyes. He breathes hard. Going to the next shelf, he realigns the other stones and glass in exact patterns. *How can he remember?*

Finished, he stands in the middle of the room and follows Hank's every move as he digs the open-topped bus more quietly under the pillows on Wilbur's bed, then to the floor where he makes screeching hairpin turns on carpet squares and comes to rest at Maggie's feet. "I'm going to like living here," he says.

Wilbur coughs, his arm bent at his chest. A painful-looking hack.

Hank lifts his arm. "I have to cough in my elbow." He pulls it across his own mouth. "Like this."

"Right." Wilbur gives him a scowl. "I'm changing clothes." He ducks behind the bathroom curtain. "Don't touch the soup cans."

With her left hand, Maggie unlaces her boots and slips into the wing tips. Her fingers still hurt under the last of Wilbur's Band-Aids as she makes a bow.

Twenty minutes later, Wilbur, in panda PJs, spoons soup into two bowls. He passes them to Maggie and Hank, the two of them sitting on Wilbur's bed.

"Wilbur, you keep the bowl."

He holds up his hands. "This won't work."

"We'll get more bowls," Maggie says.

Wincing, he shakes his head. "No, the boy. They'll hunt him. They'll find him." Wilbur coughs, hands on his knees, his body wracked. "They'll find us."

"And do what?"

"You'll be fine," he says. "But what about me?" Standing straight, he drinks his soup from the pot. "Kidnapping's a crime. No comfy mental hospital; they'll put me in prison."

"You didn't kidnap," says Hank, his eyes alight. "I *want* to be here."

"They'll say I kidnapped you both. Life without parole. You've got to go."

"We'll tell them the truth," Maggie pleads, her soup forgotten. "You saved me."

"Truth doesn't set people like me free."

"But…"

"You'll make me lose what little home I have." He scrapes the pot. "Is that what you want?"

Never. She'd never deprive him. She knows his fright. But she can't leave. The loss is hers as well.

"You would do that?" he says. "Make me truly homeless?"

Maggie has a place to go. She only feels homeless. Wilbur would have nothing.

She bends her head. She and Hank trade guilty sighs. Hank concentrates on a pen he found, and draws blue flames up his arm, overlapping a faded dinosaur.

"Finish your soup." Wilbur coughs till he retches. "Off the bed, Hank, I'm turning in."

"It's early." Hank checks his batman watch. "Not yet five."

"Doesn't matter, I'm wrung out." Wilbur's eyelids droop. Head on the pillow, he stretches out. Sweat beads his forehead.

Maggie dips a cloth in water and mops his face. "I'm worried," she tells him, the cloth turning hot on his brow. "You belong in the hospital."

"Do you hear yourself?" He gives a weak laugh. "You sound like your kids."

She can't laugh. "This is different." She gets louder, as if volume will increase his understanding. "I'm serious." She holds onto his arm. "I can't leave you." *Can't leave and can't stay.*

"You can. They'll separate us anyway. You have to go." He takes her hands in his. "We're all safer that way."

"Wilbur," she says. "I love you."

"I'm too old for this." Wilbur stifles another cough. "Love hurts." He splays his fingers across his breastbone.

"Shh, listen," she whispers.

Voices come through the furnace room wall. "God damn raccoons." Something clangs the wall. A woman's voice says, "That won't help."

Wilbur's cough doubles him up.

"That's no raccoon," a man's voice says.

"Oh, Jesus," the woman shrieks. "Call the cops."

"Go now!" Wilbur urges them out with his hands. "You can't wait."

"Go where?" Maggie struggles to her feet. She twists her fingers. Her eyes search the room.

Wilbur groans. "You have a place, your kids...."

My kids?

"Oh God! Clair!" Maggie yells in a frenzy. "My baby, she's home alone."

Fists to her mouth, she screams. "What have I done?" She snatches the mink off the bed. Her eyes roll one end of the hidey-hole to the other. For a second, she stands blank. *My purse?*

No purse. She digs in her coat pockets. No house keys, no car keys. She has to run, her heart already racing ahead. "Rog, come on."

"Nana, I'm Hank." Her Boy-Chick holds the tail of her coat.

"Mommy's coming, Clair." She'd left her... "Oh God, oh God." Starving.

Withered with thirst. For...days? Weeks? *Could it be?*

"Dear God, no—"

CHAPTER 27

MAGGIE

Friday Night

Wilbur gives a dispirited wave from his bed as Maggie, on hands and knees, scrambles across the shag and under the curtain. Into the chill evening, and with no kneepads, she doesn't feel the rubble under her knees. Her Boy-Chick follows to the sidewalk.

She knows her way home. Knows it as well as the back of her hand. She looks at her hand and frowns, turns it over and holds it up to the light, narrow fingers splayed, knuckles enlarged, blue veins that sometimes bulge as if they might burst. Today they look like blue ditches running down her wrist next to tendons straight and strong, and all webbed with crinkled skin. Her mother's hand? And no rings. The whiter band of skin on her left ring finger itches. *Robbers? Robbers in the house.*

Clair—

Heart banging, Maggie rushes the wide intersection. *My street, where's...* Street letters jumble together. *Tredbot? Trednot? Tremont?* Everything flashing—black to white to full color and back. She clutches Boy-Chick's hand.

Bicyclists zing. Cars in her crosswalk blast horns.

Lights in stores go out. *Closing.* Security grills rattle to the ground. *Tick, tick. Closing.*

Light snow begins. A hurry of pedestrians jams the sidewalk as a briefcased man bumps her.

"Hey watch it," says Boy-Chick, pushing him. She leans, and behind her, a set of hands has her by the ribs, squeezing until it hurts, sliding under her arms the way they might pick up a small child to toss it in the air. "Sorry," a man says, turning her loose. "Don't want you falling." He straightens her coat.

"My Clair... We've got to get home." She keeps tight hold of Boy-Chick and hurries, peering through a smatter of softly falling snow.

Night presses the rooftops. Maggie leans into the rush of flakes salting brick walls. Batting at the flakes, she rushes block after block, headlights, streetlights, stop lights, blinding her; police lights red and blipping, you better bloody-well-stop kind of lights.

Palms out, she takes three steps forward, one sideways, two in retreat. Three-one-two, three-one-two, her off-kilter waltz marks cryptic messages in the snow, the city a din in her head.

Hurry. She curls her shoulders, a hot prick at the top of her spine, the rest of her cold. Choked on exhaust, she turns from one street to the other. "Rutland?"

Moths claw the bars of her ribcage. Wings beat-beating. Her breath compressed. Streets go murky, intersections underwater-wavy. She hunches. Her lungs snatch at the air.

Breathe. Five, six, seven, she tries straightening.

A little hand at her elbow. "Nana, you OK?"

Breathe in. "I think so." *Out.*

Letters coalesce to names: Canton, West Newton.

"Yes." Yes, she sees it, West Newton, to.... "There it is, Rutland Square." She hugs Boy-chick. *Almost home.*

"Look Nana, the library." Lights through plate glass windows call welcome. Hank skips in place. "Ma played here when she was little. You showed me, remember?" He pulls Maggie's furry sleeve.

"Closing," Maggie says. *Closing.* The word drips in her head.

Hank nods at the big windows. "No, it's not closing." People inside busy-about in the bright room. "Let's go in."

"Not closing?" She looks through the windows. *He's right.*

All that worry over closing. *What was that?*

"No worries, Nana."

Home is in spitting distance. And Clair? Clair's with a babysitter. Maggie would never leave her alone.

"Yes, plenty of time. Let's go in."

Boy-Chick pulls her into the warmth, the scent of old paper and paste and newly laid carpet, so restful. Shelves line the walls, and half-height dividers offer a rainbow of enticing books. Her fingers itch to pluck exotic fruits.

"Hi, Linda," Maggie calls with a twiddling wave. The librarian, busy at the desk, gives her a distracted smile.

Odd, how different the place looks, the curved window seat studded with multicolored pillows.

"Nana!" Boy-Chick nudges her toward a line of tables.

When did they get computers?

"Can I play?" he asks.

"Read first. *Where the Wild Things Are?*" She heads straight back to the children's section. *Boy-Chick loves it.*

"What's your pick?" she asks.

"Night in the Museum, that's for me.

"OK. Yours is long, so I get two."

He goes to the desk. "Where can I find…"

"Meet on the cushions," she calls over her shoulder.

₮₯

Books in hand, they snuggle into the window-seat.

"My choice first, it's shortest," Maggie says, and she reads aloud in a soft voice.

Just as the wild things surround Max in the forest, a hoard of teens swarms in the door. One boy shouts, "Where's the porn?" They all shriek with laughter.

The librarian gives them a two-handed hushing, but her words can't be heard above the racket.

"What's porn?" Puzzlement crimps Boy-Chick's forehead.

"Nothing you'd like. It's not your cup of tea. Yet."

"Oh, that." He squirms. "Nana, let's find quiet."

"It's a deal."

Pillows under each arm, they take the stairs to the second floor's blissfully empty meeting room. Fresh carpet here too, with a huge brown and red oriental on top. Two plate glass windows fill one wall, pictures on the others, stacked chairs in one corner, an alcove with filing cabinets. Square lights in the ceiling give the room a sunny feel.

"Here, let's pile up the pillows." They hunker into a corner farthest from the stairs. Her legs out straight, Maggie starts again reading *Wild Things*.

Then with Max back in bed, Boy-Chick gnaws on Maggie's wrist. "I could eat *you* up."

"Not if I get you first." She flings her minky arms around him, nuzzles the back of his neck, and they wrestle, falling off the pillows. Maggie is out of breath, "I give, I give." She flops spread-eagle on her back. He jumps to his feet, arms up, making mighty biceps. *You have to look hard, but they're there.*

"I win," he crows. "Now, *Night in the Museum*."

Back on the floor, he flips through the pages. "Here." He stops at a dog-earred page. Someone else likes it as much as he does. "The T-Rex chase." He hands her the book, and they settle close on the pillows.

Well into the fifth scary scene the lights blink. "Oops, time to go."

"But we haven't got to the bad guys yet."

"We will tomorrow."

"No, Nana, tonight. Let's stay the night."

"In the library?"

He presses his hands together as if he went to Sunday school. Which he doesn't. "Special treat," he says, sweet as a choirboy. "Overnight, just like Larry and Nick in the museum."

"Aren't you afraid? What about dinosaurs?"

"Coming alive?" Up on his knees, he claps his hands. "I hope so! Besides, I have a secret weapon." He pats his cape-covered hip.

The lights blink again, followed by footsteps on the stairs.

"Nana, hide," he whispers.

"Where?" The room's too open.

"Between the files." The rug silences their scurry as they press into the small space and crouch against cold metal.

The alcove is on the same side as the door; anyone glancing in can't see them. "All fingers crossed?" They hold their breath. Maggie shuts her eyes.

"All clear," a man's voice calls from the door.

They stay crouched. "You think he's gone, Nana?"

"He better be, or my legs'll break."

Back on the pillows, Maggie rubs her chest.

"Nana, is it your heart pain?"

"It'll pass."

"You need dynamite?"

"No pills; rest is best."

"You fix yourself? That's amazing."

"Not as amazing as you," she says and presses his nose.

She ignores the crawlies, and retrieves their books. "Let's read *Charlotte's Web,*" she says. "If things are coming to life, I'd rather pigs than dinosaurs."

"How do you feel about spiders?" He wiggles in deeper.

"As long as it's Charlotte."

In the middle of the County Fair, the room goes black.

"Nana, I can't see!"

"Me, neither."

"Too bad," says Boy-Chick, "'cause I gotta pee."

"Can you wait?"

"Not long."

"Oh dear." She hikes onto all fours and then up, patting her way sideways. "Stay to the wall." At the corner, she feels the doorway."

"Hey," he says. "I can see." He takes her hand.

The big windows glow gray, but light doesn't reach into the stairwell.

"Hold the rail," says Boy-Chick. "Now the other hand on my head." He backs down the stairs. "Slowly, slowly."

By the bottom step, the yard lights reach into the hall. Maggie scans the closed doors. "'Men', there you go. Wash your face and brush your teeth, a paper towel works."

All ready for bed, they carry more pillows up to the big room and make two nests. Their coats serve as sleeping bags. Like camping, except for central heat. *What luxury.*

All cozy, they trade stories of creatures coming to life, and Boy-Chick drifts off in the middle. Maggie succumbs soon after.

‟⌘

Out of the dark, a baby's cry sits her up. "Clair!"
Did I feed her? Tonight? Last night?
Maggie scrambles for the stairs. Hardly a hand to the banister, she follows the cry down and out the door into the street.

Asleep at the library—*how could I. What kind of a mother...
My babies!*

Footsteps loud, she hurtles down avenues, down alleys, rabbits around corners, street after street. Mothy-mink coattails flap at her legs, long legs wrapped in a riot of color, feet fast in oversized wingtips. Her cheeks wet with wind-driven snow, she pants, breath thick as fog.

Flying wing-tips drum the sidewalk, Dear Dan is close. The racket glances off townhouse brick, wall-to-wall Victorians towering around her. The houses so like her own. *Mine, but...*
They rise five stories, corniced-crowns lost in the snow.

The familiar melts slippery beneath her feet, and panic pricks her chest, her head clogged, senses as slow as boots running through pudding.

She clamps gloveless hands over her ears. Her heart pounds labyrinths in her head.

The wingtips slip. She staggers, grabs the closest wrought iron fence protecting icy yards. Hand over hand, house to house, holding snow-covered rails, she squints one entry to the next, dim lights bluring the numbers.

Maggie's house, *Number five.* She squints. Not this one, not... and finally, *Yes, five,* her doorway. Light spills through etched glass in the wood-paneled door. *Home.*

She eases pent breath. *My keys.* And pats the left pocket. Access is simpler when she wears the coat right-side-out.

She pats the other pocket. *Damn, no keys.* Dan will have a conniption.

And my babies?

Late! An hour? A day? How long had she been... Murky nights fade in the glimmer of home.

She rushes up granite steps, jabs the doorbell with her thumb. Once. Twice. She bangs her fist on the glass. *Where's the sitter?* "Clair!" she shouts, "Rog!"

She cups her eyes with blue-veined hands and peers through the beveled glass, past the distorted vestibule, down the hall to hazy lights in the dining room. Off to the side, an orange glow lures her. *Someone lit a fire.*

She flashes back to evenings reading cozy by the fire (*Good Night Moon, The Wizard of Oz, Night in the Museum, Lord of the Flies*), she on the sofa, Clair on one side, Rog on the other, flames whispering behind polished andirons, the marble surround no longer smoke blackened.

For every layer of soot she removed, she'd lost layers of skin off her fingers and palms. The huge mirror above the mantle, that was a different matter. High and wide as she is tall, and framed in gold leaf, the antique she'd found on the sidewalk, pristine, leaning against a no-parking sign. It took two of them, she and Dan, to carry it home. *Oh, the treasures to be had on the sidewalk...*

But a fire now? Dan couldn't be home, not yet. She bangs harder on the glass. Her babies, could they start a fire? Would they? She and brother Bobby had, when they were little.

Gasoline, his experiment in a Mason jar. Lit, the silent blue flame remained innocuous till the jar cracked, gas flowing the length of the kitchen wall; outside, luckily. They didn't count on water spreading the flames as if they'd hosed more gas. You can't tell what kids will do, even the sensible ones.

Hurry. Fires need screens. She'll break the glass if she has to.

The door quakes beneath her fists, and from inside a shadow approaches, blotting out the light. A blurry face appears, nose to the other side of the glass. *The sitter, oh yes.*

The old one's so bossy, Maggie hopes it's the young one fiddling with the lock. But no, these days, the young one refuses to sit, frightened by junkies camped in the vacant house next door; them and the leering portraits in the dining room. They frightened her more. Maggie shouldn't have mentioned the snippets of hair in envelopes behind each painting.

The tumblers clunk. With a squeal of hinges, the door swings in, revealing a tall woman, black velvet pants and a silk top. She retreats onto the hall's Oriental runner as Maggie surges past in a shower of snow.

At the base of the curved stairway, warmth envelops her. Only a hint of moth repellant rises off her furry shoulders. She closes her eyes and soaks up the stronger scent of wood smoke. Her fingers caress carvings on the newel post.

The house hugs her.

Steam radiators give a reassuring hiss, and the last bit of panic dissolves.

"May I help you?" the woman says.

Maggie's eyes pop open. She recoils, breath sharp on intake. "You're not the sitter." Panic resurrects.

In the living room, logs snap on the hearth. "Where's Clair?" Maggie's cranky knees flex ready to... "What, what have you done with Rog..."

"I'm sorry," the woman says with unnerving kindness. "We have no Clair here." She rests gentle fingers on Maggie's sleeve. "And no..."

Maggie trembles. "No Rog?" Her voice rises in disbelief. She grips the woman's arm. "You're teasing. They're upstairs in bed." In a bound, she takes the first carpeted step. A call from the dining room stops her.

"Doris, who is it?" A man turns in his seat at the head of the table full of strangers, forks stopped half way to their mouths. They stare in silence.

"Lordy," Maggie says. "Guests for dinner?"

CHAPTER 28

CLAIR

Friday Night

Home from the lawyer's office and in the kitchen, Clair whacks chunks of beef with a cleaver. At every stroke, her blade gouges the cutting board. Rage pings red spots behind her eyes.

"Spit it out," says Roger. "The silent treatment won't help." She hadn't said a word all the way home.

"If I do, I might kill someone." She shakes the bloody cleaver at him.

If she had her way, it would be Dawn's blood. Dawn, the one who let Mum slip through her fingers. They'd been in front of the woman's desk; Mum and Hank, safe. And she let them go. With a stranger!

"If the police stop looking, it's your fault, Roger." She brandishes the clever higher. "Thanks to you, they think I'm the crazy one."

She lowers her voice imitating his man-to-man with the officer taking their statements, "My sister's overwrought. I'm sure he's a friend."

"Mum was fine." He puts out a calming hand. "She wouldn't put Hank in danger."

"But Mum and Hank, they didn't show up at the closing and they never came back to the lawyer's office. They're still out there—somewhere." Clair whacks down the cleaver. The blade quivers in the cutting board. "A 'lark,' you called it. Hank missing is not a lark! And with a strange man to boot!"

What will she say to Ben, to Sasha? If only Jeremy wasn't at Curry House, doing Roger's job.

The phone rings. She leaps for it.

In an instant, her rage bleeds out. Fear clogs her throat. What if...

Old nightmares flash, the way life replays in anticipation of death. She won't answer the phone, so no evil can squeak through the line. The one ring goes on and on...

Or good news. Damn that girl. How could she... Rage boils again, her cheeks hot.

Roger reaches for the phone. She knocks him aside. "Hello, hello?"

"Clair Mason? This is Sergeant..."

"Yes, yes, have you..."

"We've found..."

"Oh, thank god, you found them." Her breath eases in waves. "Where? Where are they?"

"Not them, Ma'am. The unidentified man in his squat."

"His what?"

"His hideout."

"And they're there. I'll come..."

"No, ma'am. Mrs. Colton and your son aren't here, just a homeless man. He's been arrested."

Fresh panic blooms. "Make him talk."

"He swears he's never heard of them. And I'm sorry, this is the worst part. We found a hospital johnny and an ID band. The band has your mother's name."

"But, that's good. It proves they were there. They have to be close."

"Yes, ma'am, but there's a lot of... of blood. On the johnny."

Clair drops the phone. She clutches at the counter; the cutting board, cleaver, and meat fall to the floor. Black speckles encroach at the edges of her vision, a high-pitched buzz in her ears.

Roger slides a stool behind her. He holds her with one arm and retrieves the phone left swinging against the wall.

CHAPTER 29

MAGGIE

Still Friday Night

"I've got this," the woman says to the man in the dining room. Then to Maggie, her words soft, "Don't worry about them." She nods toward the diners.

Candles on the table flicker. The flame cores, a cold blue, reflect off silver side dishes.

"You had me worried." Maggie smiles. "So where are they?" She looks from the woman to the table full of questioning eyes. Forks lower toward plates.

"Lordy," Maggie says. "So many guests for dinner." *And what have they done with my table?*

A hand to the wall, she steadies herself. *Where are my portraits?*

"Come," the woman says. "Sit. It's no night to be out." Snow melts on Maggie's oversized shoes. She brushes the wet from her shoulders, another whiff of camphor rising, a reminder she can't place. The woman leads her into the living room.

Maggie's eyes lift to the ceiling. They take in the center medallion, and run along egg-and-dart moldings. Oh, the hours it took, ten feet up a ladder, dental tools above her head, bringing the smothered details into sharp focus, every delicate vein on every leaf in the medallion exposed, chip by paint chip, a hundred years' worth. Her hair full of its rainbow, the dust in her nose.

In front of the fire, someone had set the screen. She collapses on a striped sofa. *Nice sofa, but whose. . .* The woman sits beside her and takes her hand. "What's your name, dear?"

"So good of you to drop by," Maggie says. *What is this new neighbor's name?* Maggie shakes her head. Nothing familiar triggers a rhyme.

A violin concerto plays softly from tall speakers on either side of the bay window. *When did Dan get those?* "I wish you could meet my husband," Maggie says. "He'll be here soon."

The woman looks past the stairwell to the dining room where dark and light faces continue to stare.

Typical South End, maintaining the racial mix she and Dan feared would disappear under urban renewal.

"You'll love townhouse living," Maggie tells the woman. "Five floors, running up and down, no need of a gym. See?" She opens her coat. "You'd never know I just had a baby." She pats the flat of her spandex-plastered belly. The one-piece suit so hard to get on and off, an exercise in itself, but a blessing after the hospital johnny. Going commando isn't her style. Too airy. She frowns.

She isn't dressed for guests. She hasn't offered the woman a drink. And those people at the table? Clearly, they expect dinner.

Maggie catches the scent of curry, her go-to dinner. *Oh hell, the timer didn't go off.* She hates dry chicken. Up she jumps. The mink falls to the floor.

She's a flash of electric sunset. *Lucky Clair's not here, she wouldn't approve.*

Halfway through the dining room, she stops. Her guests have loaded plates.

Her plate, too. It waits at the kitchen end of the table. The oval-backed chair at an angle, left on the way to answer the door. "Won't you join us," she says to the woman following at her heels.

The man in Dan's seat rises, and without a word, slips into the living room. *Just like Dan, on the phone with dinner getting cold. Where is Dan?* Late to their own party, as usual.

"Sit there." Maggie waves the woman toward Dan's empty seat at the head of the table. *Serves him right.*

Irritation on the rise, Maggie gulps the last red wine in her glass, and reaches for the bottle between a silver candelabra and a pitcher of water. Nobody eats.

They all seem frozen. *Let's loosen 'em up.*

"More wine?" Holding the bottle of red, she works her way around the table filling their glasses. Her guests' eyes follow her the way the portraits always did. She wishes Dan would ask before rearranging things. It's not like him, these unilateral actions.

"Eat, eat," she says. They only pick at the chicken as they exchange glances, their wary eyes coming back to her sitting at the head of the table. Suddenly hungry, she digs in. Nothing to eat since... *Hospital egg oozing yellow.*

The curry's good, but a little sharp. She must have forgotten the apricots. She misses their mellowing syrup. *Too late now.*

At the silent table, she gnaws the legbone. *Got to say something.* Dan always generates conversation better than Maggie. *What would he say?*

She doesn't know where the Red Sox stand, so... "How about that bussing?" She doesn't want Rog bussed to Charlestown. There's got to be a better way.

Her guests stay watchful, though no one answers. *Too controversial?* Not possible. *Not this group.* She wants to flee to the kitchen.

Dessert, surely, she needs whipped cream. No matter what's on the menu, whipped cream completes it. It's sure to present itself. The icebox. She'll find it.

The minute the kitchen door swings behind her, the dining room erupts, one man's voice over the clamor, "...any minute, they'll be here."

Lordy, more guests. And no more chairs. *What was Dan thinking?* She could kill him.

A large, dark brown cake sits in the middle of the kitchen table. Dan's favorite. *His birthday?* She counts thirty candles arranged in stiff peaks of icing. *Not my birthday.*

The door swings open, and the woman enters carrying a stack of dirty dishes. "We should wait for dessert till the others get here." She scrapes the top plate into the sink.

"Oh, don't do that," Maggie says. "There's no disposal." They haven't finished the renovations. Do it right or not at all. They had to save up. Yet... *Oh look, a Wolf.*

There, where the decrepit electric stove used to be, sits a six-burner with a gas griddle, and on the opposite wall a sleek side-by-side fridge. *Bless that man.* She could forgive all the other changes. *Well, maybe not the portraits.*

"Of course," the woman says, scooping garbage away from the drain's rubber mouth. She washes her hands, and looks at her watch.

"It *is* late," says Maggie. "We can't wait, we'll serve now."

"Or we could..."

"There's no telling when Dan will get here." Maggie starts lighting the candles.

"You get the ice cream."

Dark, oh good. Dark, like the cake. It has a name that always illudes her. She could scream. *I scream. You scream, we all...* The song mocks her. *Chocolate, yes, my favorite.*

Back in the dining room, someone dimmed the lights. The cake, a veritable bonfire, is set in front of the once-telephoning man, tall, dark hair, *like Clair,* blue blazer, white shirt, and a bow tie he straightens with a swagger. For the moment all attention is not on Maggie. Everyone breaks into Happy Birthday, and the man of the hour is named. "Dear Harry."

Maggie stands by his side struggling with the top to the ice cream, as Harry takes an enormous breath, leans forward over the cake, and blows. All the candles go out. He looks smug. "Two years without a cigarette," he says. "You could do it too, Doris."

Maggie's new neighbor smirks. "Not in this lifetime."

The blown candles stand lifeless in the icing, curled wicks blackened. Harry extracts one and lays it on the plate beside the cake. He reaches for the next, and sparks re-ignite, first one candle, then another, and another around the cake.

"Fuses," Maggie mumbles. *Oh, God.*

She knows fuses. Back on the farm, Maggie with her brother, both of them clad in tee-shirts, dungarees, and high-top Keds. Bobby and his pile of gunpowder, ever the scientist, chafing his hands. A world of trouble, that boy and his chemistry set.

"Let's test it," he said, the two of them left to their own devices in their parents' old stone house. Stone, a good thing considering their gas experiment.

"In the house?" she asked.

"Outside, dummy." He flicked his blond forelock, and tucked supplies in a box under his arm—sulfur, charcoal, saltpeter, a spool of fuse, a match box.

"It's raining." She should have known rain wouldn't dampen his ardor.

He grabbed her shoulder, pushed her out the kitchen door. She dug her heels in the dirt yard, arms crossed over her head. "No, not the barn." Their big red barn, ancient wood dry as tinder.

"Tractor bay," he said. A new cement floor made it almost reasonable.

On hands and knees, they assembled a grainy mound the size of an upside-down cereal bowl. Bobby flattened the top and inserted one end of the fuse. He unspooled a line, ran it from the pile to the barn door, and cut the fuse with a pocket knife. "This should do it."

Maggie squatted behind him as he opened the matches, took out a red-tipped wooden stick, and struck it on the side of the box. The match flared. Sulphur filled her nose.

He held the flame to the white cord. It sparked and sputtered toward the powder, inching a wiggly line of ash on the floor. Half way, the sparking stopped.

Bobby stood. Stomped his sneaker. He unrolled another length of fuse, an eye to the one on the floor.

Sparks spat again. The ball of light moved forward at a stuttering crawl, and eventually into the black pile. Bobby hunkered down in the doorway, Maggie behind him. They waited.

Nothing happened.

"Damn." Again, Bobby stood.

One hesitant step at a time, he followed the burnt ash. Still nothing.

Knees locked, he leaned over the pile. His forelock hung above the gunpowder. "Crap," he said, and bent on one knee. He looked closer at the hole where the fuse had run, and *FOOSH*, the pile blew.

With a shriek, he fell backward. "WOW." On his back, he waggled his arms and legs. "Wow, Wow." He grinned at Maggie. "It worked! What a doozie."

He was not as thrilled that night in the bathroom as he surveyed his missing forelock, eyebrows, and lashes, or when Mother slathered his face with butter. "Serves you right," she said. "The whole barn could have gone." *Never mind his eyes.*

And now, Dear Harry stands over the candles. He blows sharp blasts to no avail. The candles sparkle. Thirty threatening fuses. *A bomb's worth.*

"You beast." Harry blows harder.

"Bobby, Nooo," she shouts. Ice cream carton still in hand, Maggie shoves the man's chest. "It's gonna blow," and container high, she throws herself, spandex-breast foremost, across the cake.

Chocolate shrapnel shoots in every direction. Forks clatter with plates shattering on the floor. Shrieks accompany the smash of glasses. Chairs overturn. Glass crunches under foot. Blue lights blip across the dining room walls. The doorbell chimes.

More guests? Maggie, beached on the table, hopes someone will answer the door.

With a great stomping of boots, a volley of blue-uniformed police pours into the dining room, guns drawn. "Don't anybody move."

CHAPTER 30

HANK

Still Friday Night

It's happening *here*, in the library, a live dinosaur. Nana had warned him.

A giant, it fills the room.

No escape, he scrunches against his pillow, arms crossed over his head. The jaws open. Needly teeth gleam. Little claw fingers come at him. Hank, so tasty, squirms at Dino's feet.

"Nana, Nana," he screams. He rolls from under Dino's breath. It stinks of meat. A lump at his belt cuts into his side, and he wakes.

He scrubs at his eyes. "Nana!" he squeaks. He scrambles to the middle of the room. Rocking on all fours, he blinks, his eyes sticky. He fumbles at his belt, pulls out Dad's pistol. "Where'd you go, Dino?"

Pistol pointed into the shadows, he searches between the file cabinets. No Dino.

On his feet, gun high, Hank stalks edge to edge of the room. "Help!"

With one hand, he hits the light switch by the top step. Light fills the room. He holds a hand above his eyes. No Dino.

No Nana. He pinches himself. "Ouch."

His hand says, "Police, call the Police." Hearing himself say it helps.

"Nine-one-one." He mumbles over and over, down the stairs, his hand on the cold banister.

At home, Ma made him practice pressing the numbers. She kept her finger on the hang-up thing. "Nine-one-one, now Hank, what do you say?"

"Jeez, Ma, I know, I know."

"So, say it."

Into the dead phone he said their address. So what does he say now? They never practiced a library.

Nana hadn't practiced fighting dinosaurs, either. "Where are you, Nana?"

Inside Dino? He sees her squished in Dino's belly, like a baby about to be pooped out. He knew from pictures in *Where Did I Come From*. Sasha's old book.

Oh Nana, can you breathe? He gasps for her.

"Find the switch." *Click.*

At the main desk. "A phone." He drops the pistol on a pile of papers, and pushes everything aside. "Ah, there." He grabs it.

His cape catches his hand. He bobbles the handset. Sweat drips down his side. He pokes the numbers.

"This is not a valid number," a robot says. "Please hang up and dial again."

"Cripe on a cracker." His neck prickles. He checks over his shoulder. Dino could squeeze down the stairs and jump him.

His hand jiggles. He rests it against the desk and presses nine. His tongue feels fat. He checks over his shoulder.

"Aaaah." He'd pressed nine twice.

Again. Holding his first finger stiff on his thumb, he stabs nine. Just once, good. Now "One." He presses. And again, one.

The earpiece buzzes. "Nine-one-one, what's your emergency?"

"You gotta help, Dino ate my nana." He knuckles his teeth.

"OK kid, let me talk to your mom."

"No fooling, I saw—" He ducks his shoulders. "In the library—"

The phone slips from his sweaty hand. It hits the desk.

"Nooo," he shouts at the handset. He picks it up, but the phone's dead.

Tears stream his cheeks. He swipes at the drips, then dials, his finger wet on the numbers.

"Nine-one-one, what's your…"

"Please, she's gone." He's not sure if he should whisper or shout.

"Who's gone?"

"My nana, she…" His knees jitter worse than his hands.

"It's OK, son, what's your name?" The voice turns softer. Then mumbling.

Hank's shouting now. "You gotta save her."

"I'm here. Tell me…" He sounds all quiet and cozy—friendly, like Ben before he stomps Hank's foot.

"No, please." They don't believe him. He lets the phone fall. "What's the use?"

"Oh, Nana. Poor Nana." He flops against the desk and cries.

CHAPTER 31

MAGGIE

Still Friday Night

Dear Harry and two uniformed officers, their arms hooked under Maggie's armpits, pull her off the cake. The quart of chocolate ice cream she clutches drips onto the rug. "I'll not forget this birthday," says Harry.

An officer pats her down. *Is this necessary?*

Shaky on her wingtips, she wipes icing from her face with her cuff. "Dark, anyone?" she says.

The sorting-out takes time, with one nasty cop squeezing her arm as if she's trying to escape. *He has no right.* Maggie wants to bite him, but resists when good-neighbor Doris comes to her rescue, pushing between Maggie and the cop.

"She's not a criminal," Doris says. "Don't you dare treat her like one." She dabs a tea towel at the slurry of cake, icing, and wine adding new swirls to Maggie's neck and spandex.

"She's someone's mother," says Doris. "You better believe they're frantic."

The nice officer, protective hand to the top of her head, slides her into the squad car's back seat. She'd fought to keep her coat inside out. A conspiracy, the nasty one seemed to think, as he checked her pockets for a second time.

From the car, Maggie stretches beseeching arms toward Doris. *My babies!*

"I'll keep watch." Doris waves from the steps.

"Upstairs," Maggie shouts as the car door slams, "Top floor." Boy-Chick and his big sister in bed. She wishes she could kiss them.

"Please, sit back ma'am," says Sargent Nice. Another policeman climbs in beside her, reaches across, and pins her to the seat with his shoulder. Groping at her bottom, he trusses her up.

"Of all the…" She swats his hand. "Would you treat your mother like this?"

"Yes, ma'am, my mother always wears a seatbelt, and if she doesn't, I buckle her in." He steps out of the car. "She's set." He slams the door and thumps the roof of the car.

The seatbelt's too tight. Maggie would love to see her old neighbor Gill trussed up like this and crammed into a squad car, for what he did to Rog. Her lawyer couldn't wait to dismember the creep. Easy as pulling wings off a fly; she'd imagined it often.

A public trial? Forget it, Roger had said. *"But how? Rog couldn't.*

ଧଓ

That afternoon, high school over, Roger and Jeremy chased each other in circles at the bottom of the yard. First Rog had the hose, thumb over the male end, the spray soaking Jeremy's clothes tight to his body.

Maggie, on the phone, watched from an upstairs window as they laughed and shouted and galloped, veering in their elaborate dance. Childhood abandon, such a wonderful thing.

Jeremy tore off his wet shirt, then hopped out of his pants as he ran. Doubling back, he scooped the long hose from the ground and whipped the end from Roger's hand.

Full-pressure waved the hose, spurting water everywhere, soaking until Rog tore his clothes off too, and the game continued, both of them naked. Cocks-of-the-walk, they cavorted, splashing in a growing puddle. Suddenly the water went slack.

The hose now in Rog's hand drooped. "Hey." The boys turned to the faucet.

They froze as Gill bellowed, "You little faggots, shame on you." He snatched the hose and whaled on Rog, beating him with the metal end until red welts broke open.

200

Maggie ran screaming from the house, down to the garden, phone above her head ready to clock Gill. But he grabbed her arm and twisted, spinning her into a straightjacket hug, her back to his front. He buried his face in her neck, she, too stunned to move, and he kissed her. "This is how it's done, you fuckers." He kissed her again, shoved her at Roger, and stomped back to his house.

❧❧

Maggie unsnaps the belt, and tilts on the plastic seat as Officer Nice brakes at the corner. He turns up Columbus Avenue. Officer Officious rides shotgun, Maggie fenced off behind them. She winds her fingers in the metal lattice, muscles taught.

Over her shoulder, she watches through the rear window. Home fades in the snow, and a chill invades the car.

She folds her legs onto the seat, curls into her mink coattails, hands stuffed in opposite sleeves like a muff. *Cozy as a grizzly.* The car hits a pothole, and a lump in her coattail gouges her calf. She works it aside, and nestled in increasing warmth, her breaths lengthen.

At the station, the policeman's radio squawks like a Mynah bird on his shoulder. Maggie hears the words but they don't gel as the men escort her through the metal gateway. An alarm goes off.

"My gun," the officer says holding his pistol high, and in they go to a room with cluttered desks, people seated behind and beside.

It's hard to tell who's who by their clothes, except for uniforms who don't sit. They escort the drunk and the cuffed to a big cage, while Maggie, flanked by her escorts, sits beside an empty desk.

"In here," someone calls from a side room to a gaggle of cops hustling a shackled man through the metal detector; panda pants and bare feet. *Poor guy.*

At the same time a pretty someone wearing red, red lipstick gets prodded to the desk next to Maggie. With a smile, the woman nods at Maggie's escort. "Rough day at the office?"

"Birthday party," Sargent Nice says. The man behind Miss Pretty's desk lets his eyes amble from her red spike heels, *matches her lipstick,* up slender calves to thighs she crosses for his convenience. He continues his tour of... "Hey, Bubba," she says. "That'll cost you." She winks at Maggie.

"You've got nice legs," Maggie says. She believes in truth.

"Thanks, Grammy, I bet you clean up swell yourself."

Maggie touches her hair, stiff with dessert. Much as she likes chocolate, a shower would be nice.

"Leave her be, Bernice," says a man-boy taking the seat opposite Maggie. "She's not in your league."

"Yeah, how did you sleuth that one?"

"Age maybe."

She sneers. "Too busy with the body stocking, I bet you missed the coat."

"Looks like silk," Man-Boy says. "But so does rayon."

"Inside, Dummy. The fur, it's Blackglama."

Glama, rings in Maggie's head. *Glama-Roseanna-Danna-banana's Gramma.*

"Name?" Man-Boy demands.

The question, a simple word she can't decode. Words once at her beck and recall drop dry and useless on the floor. She licks icing from between her fingers.

Man-Boy taps his finger on the desk. "Ma'am." He sighs and rolls up the sleeves of his white shirt. "I'm Detective Strout." He poises fingers over his keyboard. "Your name, please. Now." His high-color cheeks look so like a rainbow fish.

"I caught a trout, once," she answers. "Like eating needles."

"Please, ma'am." He looks over the top of his glasses. "Who is the President of the United States?"

"You don't know?" she asks.

His lips compress. He twists a fat wedding band around his finger.

"Too bad you're married. My daughter…"

ঞ ৪

Boys always liked Clair. She could have had her pick, Yalies, Princetonians, Harvardians, but no, she had to pick Rick. OK, he went to Harvard, but Maggie could tell that the boy was disaster from the get-go. He fancied himself a rock star.

She held her tongue until the night she'd been to one of his gigs. She could overlook the seedy venue; pay no attention to the unwashed as she ordered from the bar. The neatest thing about Rick's friends was whiskey in the glass, not the passing of hand-rolled cigarettes they licked before lighting.

As the band twanged, shy Clair hung at Rick's table while other groupies writhed before the stage, liquid as cats in heat.

Rick, strutting on stage, canceled Maggie's hope for Clair's happiness. His gyrations, as labored as cranking a Model T, couldn't ignite a decent career.

The groupies didn't seem to mind, making the most of their own heat-seeking movements, honest if embarrassing. Simplistic-Rick had embarrassing down pat, but no rhythm. Maggie left early.

At two in the morning, Clair breezed into Maggie's room, and bounced her bottom on the edge of the bed, excited as when she was six. "What did you think, Mum? Mum, isn't he something?"

Maggie struggled from the depths of sleep. She forced up her eyelids, shielding against the glare from her bedside lamp. "Clair?"

Tasting too many whiskies and an overlay of toothpaste, Maggie propped herself on one elbow. She'd ordered the second whiskey hoping to mellow the effect of Rick's performance. It hadn't worked, and she ordered the third. The beer chaser was a mistake.

Clair radiated wishful expectations riding on a thick foundation of scotch. "Well, Mum? Well?"

"He's something, all right," Maggie said.

Clair shook Maggie's hip through the covers. "We're engaged," she crowed. She held up the ringless ring-finger of her left hand. "As soon as he gets paid, isn't that fantastic?"

The child should have known: to wake her mother would elicit an answer unsullied with tact. "Trust me," Maggie said, "the only ring he'll give you is ringworm."

She shouldn't have said it, and it turned out not to be true. He did give her a ring, and not from a Cracker-Jack box. A real one.

Clair would have been better off with ringworm.

ଓଓ

In the silence, Strout sighs. "Please, just answer the question, ma'am."

There's that word again. *Just.* It's never what you think. A cigar is never just a cigar, especially when someone pokes you with it.

Though Maggie knows the answer, she also knows it's a trick question.

"The president is…" *Shoot.* She can see the name, W… W… She squinches her eyes, sees the bumper sticker: Shrub for President. Triumphant, she shouts. "Shrub."

"Another for Bridgewater," says a man at the next desk. "The third one tonight, must be a full moon. What's she in for?"

"Home invasion, destruction of property, resisting arrest."

"Hang on, Boss," says Sargent Nice. "I'll check missing persons."

"What's this, a hunch?"

"Some old lady slipped her kids at the General; I'll check. See if she turned up."

"Sarg, get serious. Did you look at her?"

He's not a very nice trout.

"It won't take long."

"So do it, but hurry up."

"Check the coat," says Miss Pretty. "Betcha her name's sewn in."

The Sargent leans close. "You're right, there it is on her coat, Laura W. Helmsworth."

A man at a different desk types at his computer. "Nothing here."

"Prints," says Maggie.

"Now she's a Prince." Strout shakes his head. "Get her out of here."

"I've a…I've a…" Maggie lifts her hand, forefinger pointing at the detective, her thumb cocked. "Bang," she says. "Prints."

They're on record. She has a permit for possession and a license to carry. It's all in her head in perfect order, but she can't shake it loose. Which is worse, knowing the words that won't come, or not remembering?

"Add threatening an officer." Strout hooks his thumb toward the cage. "Now, God damn it, in the tank."

Knees together, Maggie sits demurely on a bench next to a pierced and tattooed girl. The girl scowls.

"Does your mother know you mutilate yourself?" asks Maggie.

"Shove it, Gram." The girl elbows Maggie to the end of the bench, the hem of her coat making a soft clunk against the wood. The clunk nudges her. Talks to her.

She feels along the edge to the talking knot. Through the fur, her fingers can't hear, but through silk the voice is clear. *Mother's pistol. I'm saved.*

She turns her back to the girl and pulls the knot onto her lap, attacking the seam between silk and fur, the way she'd open a bag of chips. The ancient cloth eases enough to slip a finger in. The muzzle of the pistol gives her a cold kiss.

Once she enlarges the hole, and gets the thing out, she has maybe five shots. She doesn't want to kill anyone. Getting away, that's all she wants.

Think. Think.

Face in her hands, she closes her eyes. *Envision yourself free.* If she had ruby slippers, she'd click them together. *Don't hesitate.*

With a click of her wingtips, she enlarges the hole, and the muzzle's one dark nostril emerges. She swaddles the pearl-handled beauty, careful not to let her finger enter the trigger guard, Maggie the proud mother of a bouncing baby Colt-25.

She hunkers over her tiny bundle. Protective. Fearful.

The tattooed girl sneezes. The noise leaps Maggie to her feet. She bobbles the pistol.

A gasp comes from her fellow incarcerates. They'd never have seen the pistol, small enough to fit in her hand, if she hadn't been startled.

Facing them, she backs against the bars.

"Granny's got a peashooter," she hears from outside the cage.

Next thing she knows, sets of arms cable her to the bars—ankles, elbows, knees, hips, chest. A hand easily takes the pistol from her fingers as the door opens, and cops drag her over to Strout's desk.

"Get her prints," he says.

"No need." The Sergeant, his face blank, slaps a flyer on the desk. "Margaret, known as Maggie," he says. "Mrs. Helmsworth Colton checked herself out of MGH four days ago."

"Can't be," says Trout. "Probably stole the coat."

"I did no such thing." Maggie huffs.

"Let's start again." Strout grits his teeth. "Name?"

Maggie points at the flyer.

"Didn't a squatter kill her?" Strout asks Sergeant Nice, and taps the paper.

"Found him with a bloody johnny."

"Right, they've been working on him."

"Who?" says Maggie.

"A friend of yours?" says Strout with sudden interest. "An accomplice?"

"That's him now." The Sargent turns to the other end of the room.

A gurney, guided by two EMTs, rolls toward Maggie and the exit. She stands for a better view. Under the white sheet lies a lumpish body, balding head, the face partly obscured by an oxygen mask.

"Wilbur?" Maggie throws herself at the gurney, able to snag only the sheet before an officer restrains her. The sheet slips to the floor and there he is, shivering in panda PJs. "Wilbur," she cries. The officer holds fast as the gurney bangs out through the exit and into the teeth of more shouting. Against the tide, a buzz-cut man fights his way in.

"Where is she?" he yells. Knees bent, he's ready to spring. "Where's my mother!"

Maggie hardly recognizes the face. Not that she doesn't know who Roger is; she does. But his face. The wreckage.

Maggie sees the nights and days of her absence written gray on his skin, in the bruising under his eyes, the furrowed forehead. Red lines spider the whites of his eyes, his pupils deep and black, the whole of him disheveled.

Two policemen pin his arms at his sides. He twists in their grip, his eyes wild around the room. "Mum!" he shouts. His eyes bounce from desk to desk, passing over Maggie and on to the next. "Where is she?"

Suddenly, attention returning to Maggie, he stops struggling. "Mum?" His eyes big and agonized. "Oooh, Mum." He blinks, seeming to absorb the fact of her. Finally believing, he breaks free and throws his arms around her, like the child he used to be. The child she hadn't protected enough.

"You had me so scared." He lifts his head, tears in his eyes. "Don't ever," his mouth tightens, "*ever...*"

"Mum." A shout from the entrance.

Everyone swivels as Clair shoves through the maze of desks, pushing people aside. Papers fly in her wake. Her eyes snap. Her hollow cheeks flush red.

Maggie knows the rising color. She knows the heat, how relief battles rage, but she doesn't wait for words, rage written in Clair's every fiber.

She charges. "Where is he?" She latches Maggie's lapels. Shakes her. "Mum! Where is he?"

"Where's who?" Maggie's mouth falls open.

"Hank. For God's sake, you took him."

"I did?" Terror flashes white in her chest, her head an empty space. Arms numb. In a sweat, her teeth chatter.

"You LOST him?"

"Easy, Clair." Roger wheedles between them. He whispers, "Freak her out and she'll never remember."

Clair crosses her arms, a good grip on her biceps. She turns to the detective. "Where'd you find her?"

"Face down in a cake," says the cop with the cuffs.

"Show a little respect," the Sergeant says. "There's a child missing."

"A kid in a blue cape?" asks a cop by the door.

Clair springs at the guy. "That's him, that's him. Where is he?"

The cop tilts his head toward the hall. "From the Library."

"For God's sake, bring him," says Strout.

Hank bangs in followed by Jeremy. "Look who I found," says Jeremy.

Clair spreads her arms toward Hank. "Are you all…"

Hank, cape flying, ducks under Clair's arms. He rushes Maggie, nearly bringing her down with a tackling hold around her hips. "Dino didn't eat you!" He looks up, no mask hiding his big-eyed excitement. "But guess what! I rode in a cruiser. Lights, whooper, the whole deal."

Maggie's mouth tightens. "Siren, you got a siren?"

"Enough of this," Strout says. "We're charging Mrs. Colton."

"You've got to be kidding!" says Roger striding to face Strout. "What for?"

"Possession of a firearm." He indicates the pistol on his desk.

Hank releases Maggie. One hand under his cape, he pats around his belt. His hand comes up empty. He mouths a bad word.

With his eyes all-innocent on the ceiling, Hank sidles to the detective's desk, eases around the corner, and casually walks his fingers along the edge. Now behind the desk, he snatches the pistol. Every cop in the room comes to attention.

Hank scrambles onto Strout's chair. Pistol in two hands, he covers the room. "You're not taking my Nana."

No one moves.

In the middle of the room, Strout slowly raises his hands, palms out. "Now son, don't do anything foolish. Give me the gun."

"That's mine." Maggie waves at the pistol. "I have a permit."

"Son, let's do this the easy way." Strout extends his hand. "Give me the pistol."

"Hank," Roger snaps. "Give it over." He lunges, clamping Hank's wrists, the gun high.

"Ow, quit it." Hank fights Roger's grip.

"Everyone down." The police hit the floor, guns out.

"For Christ's sake," Clair yells. "Noooo!" She leaps toward Hank, but Jeremy, faster to his wrists, holds on beside Roger.

The chair swivels and scoots from under Hank. He hangs suspended between Roger and Jeremy, his legs running in the air.

With one hand, Roger twists the pistol.

"No," Hank wails. "We have to save her." As Roger twists harder, Hank's finger forces the hammer back, and with a flash, the pistol goes off.

CHAPTER 32

HANK

Saturday Morning

He hangs by his wrists, his fingers crushed around the pistol. Every cop is flat on the floor. Killed?

His heart races, fit to pop. Killed, all with one shot?

No, each cop grips a gun pointed at Hank. Uncle R and Jeremy stare at his pistol.

"What the hell?" Strout gets up from the floor. The others stand, too. All eyes on Hank's barrel. It burns with a steady flame.

"You could light a cigar with that," says Uncle R to Jeremy. They lower Hank to the floor. Uncle R chokes on a laugh. Or is it a sob?

Jeremy untangles Hank's finger from the lighter's trigger. It hurts.

The flame stops, and Uncle R clunks the supposed pistol on the desk. "So much for possession," he says, and makes that sob sound again.

He pulls a white handkerchief from his pocket. Wipes his face. "Jeremy," he takes a deep breath, "I hope you parked nearby." He folds his handkerchief into his pocket. "We'll take Mum to Clair's."

Nana holds onto a chair back.

"Look at her," says Ma. "She belongs in the hospital."

"No hospital." Nana shakes the chair. "Not on your life."

"You need attention; your heart."

Hank's chest has stopped banging. He takes back his breath.

"I'm fine." Nana lets go of the chair. "Soap and water, that's all I need."

Ma plants hands on her hips. "The doctor said…"

"He said rest and a pill if I need one, but no no no hospital. I'd rather die."

⁝⁃

Outside the police station, the sidewalk is white. Ma has a hand on Nana's elbow. Nana twists away.

"Clair's house or The Home," Nana says. "What a choice— arsenic or strychnine?"

Hank tugs Nana's sleeve. "The pistol, why couldn't I keep it?" he says. "It's not fair." Too bad he lost Dad's at the library.

"I'm the one with the permit." Nana takes his hand. "We could have shared it." Together they bend into the wind. Snow spots Grizzly's silk.

Jeremy unlocks the van. "You're lucky they didn't shoot us all."

Uncle R grins. "I hope Strout pissed himself. He deserved it, throwing Mum in the tank."

"He apologized," Ma says and slides behind the wheel.

"That Sergeant..." Maggie lifts a tired eyebrow. "Now, *he's* a catch."

"You can't help yourself, can you?" Ma screws up her face. "Jeremy, give me the keys."

Nana pushes Hank in the far back. "In you go." She climbs in front. Jeremy and Roger sit squashed on the middle bench.

Nana looks over her shoulder. "Jeremy, I thought you left."

"He did." Hank leans into the middle seat. "But he says the ice cream's better in Boston."

"Peach?" asks Nana. "Do you dare, Rog?"

"It's under discussion, Mum, so leave it."

"He has to swallow the pit first." Jeremy laughs.

"I don't care what kind of ice cream," Hank says. "Jeremy's here. And Nana."

CHAPTER 33

MAGGIE

Saturday Morning

Maggie watches the snow. More and more flakes stream at the windshield and blur the pines by the roadside. A white vortex holds her, she and the others—five little figures inside a snow globe, no past, no future. Maggie has a moment of peace before the notion of sleeping on Clair's futon returns.

Parked at Clair's house, they pile from the van and slog through the snow, their collars high. Lights blaze from every window.

Maggie rubs the dent in the third finger of her left hand. Sixty years she'd worn Dan's ring, and the hospital took it. Now the kids have taken everything else.

But what the hell; at this moment, Maggie's so tired, even the futon looks good. She just hopes Hank's duck isn't in the toilet.

The door swings in and there's Trumpet-Girl and Hockey-Boy wearing rollerblades. "What are you doing up?" Clair says.

"We couldn't sleep," says Trumpet-Girl. "We were worried."

Zip wades into the mix. Wagging his entire back half, a stuffed turtle in his mouth, he slides to a stop and drops it at Maggie's wingtip-toes. He rises on hind legs, front paws on her chest, and welcomes her with wet kisses.

"Hey, Nana?" Hockey-Boy skates around her, and rubber brake down, he stops. An inch taller than she is, he drapes an arm over her shoulder. "How's jail?" he says. "Did they torture you?"

"Did you confess?" Trumpet-Girl asks.

"Enough third degree." Clair kisses each child on the cheek and shoos them down the hall. Covering a smile, Ben rubs off the kiss and slaps it onto the back of Hank's neck. "Nice work, *Mr.* Major Amazing Man."

"It's way past bedtime," Clair says. "And don't count on a snow day."

"Yeah! Snow day, snow day," the kids chant.

Maggie loves snow days, but cooped up in this mêlée hour after hour? *Woof.*

"In here, Mum." Clair ushers her through a set of French doors she doesn't remember. She stops and steadies herself on the pristine doorframe.

She takes in soft reds and blues, and steps onto her favorite oriental. Bookshelves line the walls, offering a rainbow of cloth and leather bindings.

"My living room?"

"I'm sorry we couldn't bring everything," Clair says.

Maggie's heart overflows, a joyous dread seeping into her veins. Hank slips in beside her. He holds her hand as she wanders from her sofa to a wingchair facing the fireplace.

In the chair, Clyde uncurls, stretches, yawns, and jumps down. He winds around Maggie's ankles, his purr a freight train.

Maggie drops her mink on the sofa and sinks into the wingchair. She leans back with a sigh. Clyde hops lightly onto her lap, and after a thorough sniffing, settles in while she tickles his ears.

Dvorak wraps her, infusing her, every note as reassuring as Sunday morning. The Hudson River flows above the fireplace, portraits over the bookcases.

Clair rests a hand on Maggie's shoulder. "I nearly came to blows over the pictures."

"Clair?" Maggie turns breathless, dread deepening. She stumbles to her feet and reaches for Clair's hand. Clyde, pushed to the floor, stalks off with an indignant flip of his tail. "Will... will it disappear? Like the horses?"

Clair takes Maggie in her arms. "No, Mum, it's real. Come, touch." Clair leads her to the bookshelves. Maggie slides her fingers over the leather bindings.

"All yours. No one enters without your invitation."

"It's so quiet in here," Hank says, a little wistful as muted feet fade behind closed doors. "You *will* invite me, won't you Nana?"

Clair leads Maggie to the dining room. "Your bedroom," she says.

Just like home, the canopied bed, its headboard against the wall, her mother's crocheted spread smoothed over plump pillows. The highboy stands opposite, and more ancestors look on from their frames hung in spaces between the windows and doors. Gatsby waits on the bedside table where she left him, agonizing over his losses.

From the closet, Clair unhooks Maggie's flannel nightgown. "You may want a shower first."

"Mmm, my cake facial is flaking."

"And here," says Clair. She opens the coat closet and flicks on the light. Now cleared of old parkas, sports equipment, and paint, it houses a tiled bathroom including a shower with massaging heads. *And no duck.*

Maggie can't wait to brush her teeth with running water, and best of all, use a flush toilet. Not as handsome as Wilbur's chamber pot, but it beats sneaking outside.

Oh, Wilbur—What will they do with you?" Moths dance her breathless, and thankfully, on the pedestal sink, her pill waits in a dish. She holds it under her tongue.

Everyone is tucked in, but tired as she is, bed doesn't call her. Maggie stays on the sofa.

A gentle tap sounds at her glass door. Hank, in footy pajamas, green blaze on his sweatshirt, hovers in the dark hall. His hair awry, worry crimps his face.

She waves him in. "Major Amazing Man, no invitation's needed."

Dragging his cape, he sidles to the sofa, leaving the door ajar. He sits at the far end, hands and cape pressed between his knees.

Maggie pulls him beside her. "Why so shy?" She covers their feet with the mink.

Hank twists the cape with nervous fingers. "Nana?" he asks in a small voice. "Are you mad at me?"

She takes his hands and looks deep into his worried blues. "I couldn't possibly be mad at you; you saved me."

Hank gives a wan smile. "I wanted to. Amazing Man tried, but nearly got you shot, and Ma says…"

Maggie holds up a hand. "I know, 'grounded for life;' she said the same to me."

"The naughty chair." Hank's shoulders sag.

"For both of us," says Maggie.

"You, too?" He perks up. "Us? Together?"

"Yes," she says and sinks deeper into the sofa. "Comfy, isn't it?"

CHAPTER 34

MAGGIE

The Following Monday

In her four-poster, a swirl of predawn fog dims Maggie's dream of Chunky Monkey for breakfast. She sits up in the gentle glow of the nightlight. *My bed.* She pats the mattress. *My own sheets. What bliss.*

But the bed. It's displaced, much like a shoulder ripped from its socket. In disbelief she watches the fog pale to mist and dissipate, leaving her—the real Maggie, compos-mentis on the bed, palms cherishing her cotton sheets—all inside a bubble. The bubble lodged in Clair's house.

Confusion a memory, she rises, slips bare feet into Dan's wingtips, and ties the laces in a bow. She straightens the covers and pulls her mother's spread over the pillows before clomping carefully into her living room, where Hank's cape lies over the back of her sofa. Only real kids allowed at school, so says his teacher.

Funny, how clarity holds her as if she'd never had a foggy moment. She treasurers all that's left of her home, Clair's careful imitation of life.

Clair tried hard. *She did.* And she came close, all the while Maggie fighting her kindness.

As children, Rog and Clair had done the same to Maggie, her efforts at keeping them safe spurned, and so it continues, her every attempt ignored.

But of course, much as she wants it, she can't stitch Roger's rumpled skin to fit. She can't tap a wand or kiss a frog and find Clair a competent Romeo. Harder still, she can't keep Hank amazingly five forever.

And Maggie, she isn't Thumbelina, tiny enough to live a miniature version of herself. She's outgrown fairytales, even outgrown Fitzgerald.

No more chasing the past. I won't be Gatsby.

Effervescence bubbles through her, and outside in the gray dawn, snow swirls to a stop. Through the window she sees white spread wide as an ocean, distant rocks barely breaking the surface. Above them a sepia cloud hovers. *Moths.*

A chill takes her.

No bathrobe at hand, she retrieves Hank's cape, throwing the electric blue over her shoulders. She keeps a wary eye on the cloud.

The brown cumulous billows in streaks of sun, a hint of glitter lit deep in the mottle. "Not moths," she whispers, excitement blooming.

Flannel-covered arms rise. The cape flairs. "Butterflies," she shouts. And joy to the marrow, she strips the last of mothy-encumbrance, wingtips dancing her, dancing her into a world of monarchs and swallowtails.

ACKNOWLEDGEMENTS

I want to thank my children, grandchildren, and especially my mother for their constant inspiration, and to my partner Priscilla Fales for reading first, then rereading, and with enthusiasm reading again.

Thanks to Nancy Rosenblum for permission to use her words in a found poem at the start of this book; and to the secret technician at Mass General who gave me the johnny featured on the book cover.

Endless thanks go to Michelle Hoover and Lisa Borders for including me in Grub Street's first year Incubator; and to my weekly Cambridge writing group: Louise Olson, Fran Mascolo, Grace Billings, Sheila Finn, Sandra Schuman, Bette Skandalis, Hope Tompkins.

And to my whole-novel group, who tell me the hard truth, book after book despite my moving to Maine. Where would I be without you: Nichole Bernier, Kathy Crowley, Juliette Fay, Randy Susan Meyers.

And most of all, my gratitude to Frayed Edge Press and Alison Lewis who chose to publish *Loose in the Bright Fantastic*, then, with a vigilant eye acted as shepherd through every phase.

ABOUT THE AUTHOR

E. B. Moore is a metal sculptor turned poet and novelist. She grew up in a Pennsylvania fieldstone farmhouse, moved to the Boston area, and finally found a sense of home in a South End townhouse and later a loft in Cambridge. In the middle of raising her family, her mother moved in following unsuccessful brain surgery. The family coped by finding the lighter side of outlandish happenings over the eight years they lived together; these experiences partly served as the basis for writing *Loose in the Bright Fantastic*. E. B. Moore is also the author of the poetry chapbook *New Eden, A Legacy* (Finishing Line Press, 2009) and the novels *An Unseemly Wife* (NAL/Penguin 2014) and *Stones in the Road* (NAL/Penguin/Random House, 2015). She is the mother of three, the grandmother of five, and currently lives with her partner in Scarborough, Maine.